Moxxanne

and the Third Zenith

Gary Louis Rondeau

FriesenPress

Suite 300 - 990 Fort St
Victoria, BC, V8V 3K2
Canada

www.friesenpress.com

ISBN
978-1-5255-1084-7 (Hardcover)
978-1-5255-1085-4 (Paperback)
978-1-5255-1086-1 (eBook)

1. FICTION, COMING OF AGE

Distributed to the trade by The Ingram Book Company

For Marie
The Light

Chapter 1

Moxxanne stared up at the plain, but still a gingerbread, two and a half story building that was Gaylord's city hall. Definitely not that imposing, but Gaylord, having around ten thousand souls, was officially able to call itself a city, though in their hearts and minds they preferred to think of themselves as a bustling prairie town. It was winter, the fifteenth of December, snowing fluffy flakes, and the usual cold -20°C. A modest eleven concrete steps led up to the double, front doors and Moxxanne took them two at a time to a small landing, about three hundred square feet. Moxxanne did the Rocky thing and started bouncing up and down and clapping her hands over her head.

"I'm here, you lucky people!" she shouted. "I'm here among ya! So open up your hearts and let me in!"

Moxxanne was tall, five nine at least, weighed around one forty. She had silver blonde hair, big hair, and it bounced at her shoulders. Her dark sunglasses were the curvy wraparound kind and, of course, her right hand clutched a smartphone. Her black jacket was strictly biker, unzipped despite the cold, she wore tight jeans, faded ones torn at the knee but nothing looks better on a dame with a great ass and legs. It was 9:00 a.m. on a Monday morning and sleepy Gaylord was at last awake but even now there were only a few side-walk pedestrians who paused to take in the spectacle. Moxxanne kept bouncing and celebrating her arrival.

"Lucky people! I'm here, I'm here, I'm here!" Her strong soprano shout could be heard way down the block.

The city hall front doors opened and a Gaylord police officer stepped out. He had a valise under his arm and sunglasses in his hand. He let the heavy door close behind him and stopped to take in the impromptu show. Moxxanne did a few more jumping jacks and stopped.

"Good morning, officer," Moxxanne said brightly with a big beaming smile. "Beautiful day, isn't it?"

Gaylord is an unrushed and tolerant town. The police officer didn't smile; neither was there disapproval on his face. He didn't nod or acknowledge. Just that significant pause and observation. Then he put his sunglasses on and went down the steps to where his cruiser was diagonally parked. The show was over. Moxxanne had arrived in Gaylord.

Moxxanne came down the steps and started making her way to Tim Hortons where she had left her rented Mustang. The snow continued and began matting up in her silvery locks and the biker jacket was still wide open in spite of the chill. Fingerless gloves. Her fur fringed snow boots were the sensible part of her rig.

Moxxanne didn't walk so much as she pranced and danced, like some kind of celebrity who had popped into town. She offered friendly high fives to the sidewalk folks and some obliged, especially the young. She stopped and waved gleefully at the main street traffic and got some honks back in return; she was a pretty girl.

At Tim Hortons she toned it down and ordered a latte and a Manhattan doughnut. She grabbed a seat with her back to the counter, facing the street windows where she watched people and traffic. It made her happy – this was all so much what she had dreamt.

Chapter 2

He heard no sound and felt no pain. His vision was coming and going in jolting flashes. Somebody was on him, shoving him, shoving him, shoving him. Then sound came back the same way – on, off, on, off. He had both senses for four or five seconds at a time, both sight and sound.

Orson's face loomed close, the eyes wild, the mouth contorted then he heard him loudly, "Harry! Harry! Harry!"

Then the face rose up, up and he heard a terrible clamour on the stairs, as though men were shouting and running up and down. Then they were in his den; they seemed to have yellow coats? Hats? They grabbed at him roughly and shoved a mask over his face. The loud talking went on and on and he could see better now and there was Orson pointing down at him, his mouth wide, shouting, shouting, and he couldn't understand except for Harry! Harry! The big yellow-coated men were picking him up and placing him on a gurney; they already had an IV stuck in his arm. The gurney rose up, up.

Harry tried to speak, but no words came, nothing, not even a gurgle. He was conscious now has they packed him out of his den and trundled him down the curved staircase. He glanced at the grandfather clock at the landing: 10:35 a.m.

Someone had left his wide front door gapingly open, and he felt the jolts as they took him down the seven front steps onto the sidewalk. He did not feel the frigid outside air, which was minus twenty. An ambulance waited with flashing lights and back doors yawning open, showing off the garish green interior.

Harry was perfectly aware now and knew what was happening but what he didn't know was why.

Chapter 3

Moxxanne had her sunglasses perched atop her silver blonde hair while nursing a Tim Hortons latte and thumbing through texts on her smartphone. She looked up and then levelled on a man's accusatory face. She tried melting him with a toothy smile. Didn't work.

She shrugged, "What's up, cowboy? Lose your horse?"

The man was bald and with a fringe that noosed into a grey ponytail. He wore a black biker jacket much like her own, faded jeans and a black t-shirt showing over the low coat zipper. He scowled.

"So you're the brat asking around about Harry."

Moxxanne had been in Gaylord three days before making her introduction at city hall.

Moxxanne sipped her latte. The man had a bent boxer's nose to go with his truculent appearance, hands that dangled at the cuffs.

"Sit, take a load off."

He sat, big mitts on the table. "Whaddya want?" he said.

Moxxanne licked latte off her lips. "Plenty. But I don't see you on my agenda," she said with a challenging grin.

He rocked back and forth, no smile. "I'm more than you can handle, kid. You better tell me what this is all about."

Moxxanne's dark biker jacket was over the back of her chair and she was wearing a tight, fuzzy sweater. Now she leaned back to flaunt an impressive figure. "You first, cowboy. What's up your ass?"

He looked over to the counter. "Stay here, kid, I'm gonna grab a coffee."

Moments later, he settled back in and made a thing out of stirring his cup.

Moxxanne turned on a big teasing smile. "I know your name," she said coyly.

"Oh? How so?" His face was unfriendly but his eyes showed something else.

"It's Orson. You're Harry's friend. I actually do have you on my list so you're saving me the trouble of looking you up. Bet you don't know my name."

He nodded, "Sure I do. You've been dropping it all over. It's Roxanne."

She laughed, a handsome young woman, great showy teeth, "No, it's not. Try Moxxanne."

At last he smiled, taking off some age. "Moxxanne? What kind of name is that?"

She laughed, "It's mine. Okay, I changed it. It used to be Roxanne. What kind of a name is Orson?"

He relaxed, taking more age off. "Okay, kid, I got it – Moxxanne, and I know what you're up to; you're writing some kind of goddamned book about Harry."

She took a sip of latte and then licked her frothed lips before shaking her head. "Not a book. I'm doing an essay for Ryerson University."

He had light eyes and now they narrowed, "An essay? You're taking English?"

She shook her head, "Third year law. But I'm also a writer for Ryerson Press."

Orson held his coffee cup up as though he were warming his hands. Now he shook his head, "Bullshit. You're snooping around for some law firm."

Moxxanne drained her latte before speaking. "If I was, you wouldn't catch me."

Orson laughed, his eyes lighting, "You sure as hell are a brat. Too bad Harry will never get to meet you."

Her green eyes teased, "Oh, yes, he will."

Orson saw that she was very sure of herself. He put a hand to his jaw, a face that had been smoothed by many old time punches. "You do know that Harry's very ill, don't you?"

"I do. All the more reason I want to see him soon. Why don't you arrange that for me, Orson?"

He pushed back from the table, "Why the hell should I do that? Look, kid, I'm here to tell you that he won't want to see you. He's a very sick man." Her face was pretty from almost any angle.

"Orson, here's the thing. I'm Harry's niece."

Orson frowned, this news catching him unawares. "Niece? How could that be?"

Moxxanne just shrugged and smiled.

Chapter 4

"What day is it?" Harry was asking Orson at the new Gaylord General Hospital, which he knew was eleven years old, and to which he had made contributions totalling around twenty-five thousand to the building project.

"It's Monday morning, Harry," Orson told him. "You've been here since Friday morning so it's been three days."

Harry nodded; speaking was still an effort. A line carrying oxygen covered his nose and an IV dangled at his side. His face was both yellow and ashen. He had recently turned seventy-five and looked every year of it; he could pass for the late Humphrey Bogart's father. His dark eyes went to the corners so he could see the seated Orson.

"They haven't told me a thing – don't know what the hell happened to me."

Orson shook his head, a solid-looking man. Though five years younger than Harry he looked younger, more like sixty instead of seventy.

"You had some kind of heart attack, Harry. They told you, but apparently you're stabilized now so it's all good, Harry." He patted Harry's gowned shoulder with his old boxer's hand.

Harry's eyes were narrow and pleading, "Take me home, Orson I want to go home."

Orson kept patting. "Soon enough, Harry. They couldn't get all their tests done because of the weekend and all that." His hand stayed, "Oh, I almost forgot, Dr. Schiller told me you're probably going to have to go into Winnipeg to the St. Boniface Hospital to see a cardio guy and have more tests done."

"Oh, shit," Harry said weakly and shook his head. "I don't feel good about this, Orson."

Orson sat back. He was bald except for short grey hair circling at ear level, his face definitely that of an old-time boxer, all smoothed and softened by punches.

"Ah, take it easy old buddy – you're going to make it this time – don't you worry." He put a steadying hand back on Harry's shoulder. "Say," he said, his gruff fighter's voice brightening, "I almost forgot. There's this pretty young chick in town asking a lot of questions about you."

Harry managed to turn his head slightly, a question in his eyes.

"I tracked her down at Tim Hortons. She's some looker, I'll tell you. Reminded me of a young Kim Basinger." Orson had a way of leering when he spoke of attractive women.

"What'd she want?" Harry said. He was feeling the urge for sleep, but was trying to resist.

"She says she's a Ryerson student. Calls herself an investigative reporter. Says they're doing a story on you and doing background." Orson left out the niece part. Harry really didn't look strong enough to take that news.

Harry relaxed, turning his face forward. "Oh, one of them. We've had a few of those. Just keep her away from me."

Orson pressed Harry's shoulder. "I'm thinking her story is just a cover. It turns out she's a third year law student. I'm thinking she's doing some ground work for the Yukashita people. I can smell that kind of stuff a mile away."

Harry smiled grimly, "Law student? You're probably right. Make sure you keep her away from me, Orson. Don't let her into this hospital."

Orson grabbed Harry's shoulder conspiratorially, "I've got this idea about her, Harry Maybe she'd be good for you, spy or not."

Frustration showed in Harry's aged face. "No, no, Orson. No good for me at all."

Orson put his head closer, "It's the way she looks, Harry, and her personality. I sat down with her and had a cup of coffee. Damn! She was giving me a boner. She's young, probably only twenty and sexy beautiful. But it's more, Harry, it's more – she's just so healthy looking that she makes a guy feel better. They don't have medicine that good, Harry. There's nothing like a good looking young dame."

Harry closed his eyes, "You always did like 'em young, Orson. Keep her away from me."

Orson straightened, "Oh, I won't let her get in here, but once you get home, and if she's still around, I'm going to bring her over to meet you."

"I gotta get home first," Harry managed, he was falling asleep.

Chapter 5

Neither of them liked the wheelchair so they collapsed it and left it propped against the wall of the old house's large foyer. Then Orson, nearing seventy, helped his old friend Harry up the winding stairway and into Harry's office. It had originally been the home's master bedroom, but that was almost thirty-five years ago when Harry had bought the respectable, but too small to be a mansion, home. Orson eased Harry's skinny and lanky frame onto his comfortable, executive chair behind the equally executive desk. Both pieces had come out of Gaylord's old General Hospital, demolished and rebuilt twenty-five years ago. The furniture had been auctioned off and Harry had secured the desk and chair for himself. Prior to that, a not-so-modest sum of Harry's money had gone into the new hospital's building fund.

Orson patted Harry's boney shoulders.

"There you are Harry, you made it home – not dead after all."

Harry's fox-face was even more narrowed, but the eyes were dark and steady. He reached a liver-spotted hand to a humidor and fished out a cigar. After the first puff, his stained teeth clenched it with satisfaction. He twisted around.

"Orson, grab me a Gentleman Jack." Four fresh bottles were still lined up on the fireplace mantle – the remainder of a dwindling honour guard.

Orson dropped an empty bottle into the waste basket and put the new one on the desk.

Soon Harry was puffing and sipping.

Orson perched himself on the edge of the sturdy desk. "Okay, let's hear it. What the hell happened to you?"

Harry shook his head and rubbed his hand across his eyes, everything an effort for him. Just getting home in the Lincoln Town Car had further sapped his strength.

"Was it a heart attack, Harry? A stroke?"

Harry shook his head while taking another sip. "Orson, damned if I know, and damned if they know. How long was I in there – a week? All those goddamned tests. Jesus, what couldn't they know about me?"

Orson went over to a small fridge by the mantle and grabbed a beer. He preferred beer over whisky. "So what did Doc Schiller have to say?

Harry rubbed the back of his hand against his forehead.

"What the hell day is it today?" he asked.

"Monday, why?"

"Doc Schiller says they sent all the tests to a cardio guy in Winnipeg, but Schiller doesn't think it was a stroke, maybe not even a heart attack. Christ, Orson, I'm probably just old and tired and getting ready to kick. Don't be surprised."

"Surprised? When I you found here beside this desk tits up on the floor, I thought you were dead! Jesus Christ, Harry. I was about to give you the old kiss of life when your eyes suddenly popped open. Scared the shit out of me, but you couldn't speak so I dialed 911 and that was it."

Harry tapped the cigar in the ashtray, fingers long and bony. He still had a full head of lank white hair with strands of black, a few hanging over his unshaven face. He looked haggard.

"I didn't want to wake up, Orson. It would have been better. You know what a goddamn mess I'm in. That was my chance to fuck off. Should've happened."

Orson came off the desk. A middle-sized man, mostly bald but still vigorous looking. He'd been a welterweight pro boxer and it showed in his face and actions: Gaylord's folks still respected his cocky attitude and educated fists.

"Godammit, Harry, I don't want you talking like that. It's all bullshit. What does it matter if you're broke or not? You ain't dead and you gotta face up to things." He waggled a finger, "That's always been your trouble, Harry, too much fuckin' procrastination."

Harry smiled grimly, the smoky cigar in his mouth, "You got that right, I'm even procrastinating over death." He shakily drained his glass and poured another couple of fingers. "But you're right. If I'm up to it, I'll start tomorrow. I'll talk to Gerry over at the TD bank, the bastard wants to foreclose on me. Then I'll see if I can get a hold of Roger – that goddamned lawyer is not easy. I was lying in that hospital bed, I realized that it was over. I'm beat. Do you remember about five years ago when a settlement was offered?"

"Sure, chickenfeed. You laughed and threw it back in their faces." Harry butted the cigar. "That was then. I'm going to see if Roger can get that back on the table." He looked over at Orson, "How are things going at the Oasis Trailer Park?"

Orson nodded sourly, "Doable. I got a double wide after all. We'll need storage lockers for all your shit." He shook his head, "Boy, what a comedown from this place."

Harry drained his glass.

"Jesus, I'm gonna have to take a nap." He looked over to the long couch, kitty corner to the fireplace and under a bank of draped windows.

Orson perched on the desk again, "Hang on, Harry," he said, his light eyes going to the ceiling and down again, something he did when he had an issue.

Harry was long familiar with the look. "Oh, oh. What's happened now?" his chair creaked back.

Orson held up his hands, "I was thinking maybe I wasn't gonna tell you today. Maybe you should just take your nap."

17

Harry shook his head. "Can't be that bad. You already would've told me. Come on, out with it."

Orson stood up and brushed make believe spots off his white t-shirt.

"Remember I told you there's a young dame in town? And she's been asking questions about you all over the place?"

Harry jerked back, like he was going to go over, his dark eyes narrowing. "Remind me what the hell she wants—"

Orson held his hands up defensively, "Hold on. She's a reporter. Sorta."

Harry's lips twisted, "Oh, one of those. Well, don't let her near me."

Orson shifted on the desk. "You might have to see this one, Harry."

"Oh? Why so?"

"Because apparently you're related."

Harry picked up the dead cigar and clenched it. At last, he pulled it from his mouth.

"Jesus, Orson, where the hell are you going with this?"

Orson pushed off the desk. "First of all, she's a law student at Ryerson University. Second of all, they've got a campus newspaper that's sent her down here to do some kind of bullshit story about you and the City of Gaylord, and thirdly, she claims that you are her uncle."

Harry leaned back again, shaking his head wearily. "No fuckin' way, Orson." He looked up, "How could I be her uncle?"

Chapter 6

Harry's jaw, with its unshaven white stubble went up, he cast his eyes around, "I'm asking you, Orson, how in hell could I be her uncle?"

"Harry," Orson protested, "This is your relative, not mine."

Harry's thin lips stretched across his narrow face, "What relative?"

"Your niece – you know – the one called Moxxanne."

Harry flinched, somewhere in the far recesses of his mind a dim light blinked.

Orson shrugged, hands open innocently, "Not my problem, Harry. You better talk to her."

Harry let his chair creak back.

"Christ, Orson, I'm trying not to be dead. She's probably just one of these author-chasing brats. You know the ones. They want to move in and become apprentice writers." He shook his head decisively. "No, no. I don't want anything to do with her."

Orson sat down on edge of the desk and lowered his head, "Harry, now you better listen. I believe this kid really is your niece." He pointed his finger in Harry's face. "She told me she's your brother Early's kid. How in hell can you say you don't know about her?"

Harry closed his eyes and bit his lip, like his energy was shot. Slowly his eyelids came up and he waved Orson away. He shook his head sadly. "Goddammit, that fuckin' Early. But, I don't recall any Roxanne."

Orson punched a fist into the palm of his hand; he had a habit of doing that. "It's Moxxanne with an M, and two X's."

19

Orson had a way of smirking and squinting when he talked about women. "And it suits her. Boy, this kid is built, and she's got your brother's dimples, too."

Harry stared vapidly, like he was trying to imagine his brother's dimples. When he spoke, his voice was an old man's murmur. "Okay," he said, "I'll deal with it tomorrow."

He cranked his head, adding another thought, "Keep her outta my hair for the time being. Maybe you could buy her some dinner or something."

"Why sure! I'll offer her my arm." He squinted and stuck his tongue out, "They'll get a jolt when the see her at the Eagle's Club. Hey, maybe she plays pool. She's at Ryerson after all."

Harry's eyebrows raised, "Ryerson?"

"Oh yeah, no dummy this one. Third year law student. I told you this before."

Harry's eyes narrowed, "Trouble. I see trouble, Orson."

Orson stopped with his hand on the doorknob, "Oh, by the way, Josie says she'll be bringing your dinner up."

"Not hungry," Harry said, shaking his head, half-closed eyes lending him a lizard look. He pointed to the long chesterfield opposite the fireplace and India rug.

Wordlessly Orson went over and helped his old friend onto the soft couch. He propped the cushions under his head and spread an afghan over him. Orson went softly away.

Harry was asleep within moments.

Chapter 7

Harry's gnarled hand grabbed the receiver after the fourth ring and instantly recognized Larry Gannon's business voice – not the more natural one that he used at the Wednesday-night poker games.

"I'm so glad you're home, Harry. I've heard you've been having a rough time."

"Yeah. Life seems to be trying to steamroller me." Harry's voice was only a little clearer than the day before when Orson had picked him up at the hospital.

"What happened? I'm hearing heart attack."

Harry's voice went scratchy with a minor coughing spell before he could speak. "Doc Schiller isn't too sure. Something bad happened, but so far the tests haven't pinpointed anything definite."

"Oh, Harry, they gotta do better than that. I can't believe it."

"Well, thanks, Larry. I appreciate it, but I know you didn't call just to wish me well."

Larry's voice switched to his more cordial poker game tone. "It's a bitch, Harry, being a bank manager in Gaylord but, it's my job. I hope you understand that."

"Sure I do. I'd rather take your money from the poker table."

Larry managed a laugh, "Orson's done enough of that. Except for him, I'm about even."

Harry sighed wearily, "Well, at the bank, I know we're not. So, what's gonna happen now?"

There was silence for a few moments.

"Larry?"

"Oh, sorry, I was checking my computer. Harry, of course it's bad – out of my hands now. You're two hundred thousand over the cut-off and three months in arrears. I'm sorry Harry, but our regulators are taking over. Believe me Harry, my phone call today is purely to reprise you of this situation. Harry, surely your publishers can come up with, say, a five figure amount?"

"I wish, but you know all about this, Larry. I'm owed a bundle – but the lawyers still can't get us into court, so I'm afraid I can't come up with dime one."

The TD Bank manager groaned audibly, "Oh boy, this shouldn't be happening to you. it's a damn shame. These movie people have been screwing you around for what, ten years?"

"Something like that."

"Harry, look here. It's only a suggestion but I've done it in other situations. Maybe you should let me talk to your lawyer? Sometimes it motivates people if they hear it from me. You know, the urgency? Whaddya think?"

"This is Gaylord. Everybody knows everybody, so I guess you can talk to Roger if you have a mind to, but I can't see how it can do any good. Anyway, he's in Winnipeg over some big case. I'm waiting to meet with him myself."

"Harry, promise me you're gonna take some action; anything at all. Get me something so I can talk to our regulation department."

"Well, I'm trying to take one breath after another. That seems to be my main game at the moment—"

"Of course, of course, Harry. I hope you don't think I'm trying to push you. Nobody wants you to have another heart attack."

Harry managed a cackle, "Thanks, me too, but right now it seems to be a race between my dwindling resources and what's left of my life."

Chapter 8

Harry stared out the window of one of Dr. Schiller's two examination rooms, and, as usual, the wait was exasperating. He was left to suffer the doctor's drab surroundings on top of feeling lousy.

A rap at the door and Dr. Schiller peeked in, "Ah, Harry, and how are you today?"

The question didn't need an answer, so Harry just gave him a solemn nod.

Dr. Schiller placed some papers on the desk. His half glasses hung on a dark cord so that they dangled on top of his stethoscope, but now he parked them on his nose and began to sort through the test reports, laying each page gently aside. At last he dropped the glasses and looked up, rubbing a knuckle over his left eye socket. Dr. Schiller was of an age that was not far off Harry's. His full head of silvery grey hair was neatly combed in an old-fashioned centre part. Shoulders slouched, he still wore the old time white lab coat. The white moustache didn't subtract any age off his wrinkled face.

"Damn it, Harry," Dr. Schiller said, leaning back and folding his small hands in his lap. He shook his head, "The tests don't show us what's happened – not conclusively. I just hate that sort of thing. What am I supposed to tell you?"

The two men had known each other for going on thirty years, but there was no fondness between them. Respect yes, but no real friendship.

"You could tell me if you think I'm dying," Harry said.

Dr. Schiller had cold, dark eyes. Over the years he'd told too many people they were dying. He shook his head and tapped a finger on the stacked papers. "The tests don't say that – not so far. So I can't tell you that, not officially," he leaned forward, sticking his jaw out, "but I did tell you to quit drinking and smoking, Harry, and you admit that you're still at it." He paused, shaking his head in disapproval, "Yes, you're very ill, Harry, and a good part of it is your own damn fault."

For a brief moment, Harry felt as if he'd been slapped, but then the feeling vanished; it was all too true.

Harry spoke softly, his haggard, fox face breaking into a grin, "Okay, Doc, we understand each other. But, I still need your considered opinion. There's stuff I need to clean up – my will and so forth—"

Dr. Schiller cut him off with an upheld palm, "Of course, of course," he said. "You do that, but look here, nobody's giving up on you." He tapped the test results again, "The St. Boniface Hospital has informed me that all your test results have been sent to the Mayo Clinic. It's a new connection they have. If Mayo wants more tests we can provide them, or St. Boniface can." He leaned back, softening his posture. "It's December, Harry, so you're not dying this year, okay? Go home and get on with your life and let me worry about next year."

Chapter 9

It was mid-December and -20°C in Collingwood, Ontario. Patterson Printing Co. had completed all its Christmas contracts, and in a week's time the whole operation would shut down for the Yule time holidays. The much smaller Patterson Publishing side of the operation, Can-lit fiction authors only, would follow suit, but right now an important meeting was taking place in Gertrude Bachalder's third floor office. It was a meeting she scarcely expected, but heartily welcomed.

Was there to be a great Christmas present in the offing? Why did the officer from Yakushita Heavy Industries who was also the CEO of Advent Studios unexpectedly request this face-to-face meeting? Their lawsuit had been churning away for more than five years with almost no significant results. And it was all to do with the two Zenith Sci-Fi movies made back to back over twenty years ago by Advent Studios, the books for which had been contracted from Patterson Publishing.

The Zenith movies, like all Advent movies, were pretty much B-movie affairs, but here's the thing: they unexpectedly began to generate significant income, only not from North America. No, the Zenith movies just kept on growing and growing offshore, especially the Far East versions. Advent Studios enjoyed a fat income stream and, of course, Patterson Publishers shared handsomely. A third Zenith novel was contracted to complete the trilogy, but so far this hadn't happened. Reason? Twelve years ago, Yakushita Heavy Industries had bought Advent Studios, located in Hollywood, and gradually began moving most of the business lock, stock, and camera to Hong Kong.

Patterson Publishing's golden Zenith royalty stream began to shrivel and it was now almost nothing – a great loss to the company and to the author, Harry Breen. Of course, the subsequent lawsuit soon broke open and had been fizzing and hissing ever since, but to only pecuniary results. Yakushita, powerfully lawyered, had managed stay after stay of court dates. But you may only hold off the USA and Hollywood from their just desserts for so long. Early in the coming year, Yakushita was finally going to have to step into an open court, this to be in Los Angeles, and a lot of restitution was going to have to be made good. And now Gertrude Bachalder was thinking this was about to change.

The loss of income and mounting legal fees had sorely hurt a small publishing company such as Patterson, almost to the point of putting it under, and had likewise done the same to the author, Harry Breen, forcing him into a financial crisis.

Gertrude Bachalder was still trying to get it into her head that the Japanese man in the soft comfortable chair in front of her desk was actually, by his own admission, thirty-five year's old. He seemed hardly twenty-five, being small in the Japanese sense, maybe five five, and with a full head of shiny black hair neatly combed and with no part, a creamy, youthfully smooth face, the dark eyes calm, innocent. He was sitting there so quietly, hands in his lap. So, this then was the man from Yakushita Industries and CEO of Advent Studios – this dapper and friendly little fellow – but certainly not powerless.

Gertrude proffered the open box of Ganong chocolates and, again, Joisei Yakushita selected one.

"These are so good," he said. "My mother would just love them."

In an alcove of the office, a canary in a cage began to flap its wings and sing. Joisei Yakushita swivelled his neck and stared appreciatively. "Oh, you have a bird. My mother would just love that."

"It's not real," Gertrude said. "It's animatronic. Less bother for looking after."

Joisei turned back. "So, not real. My mother only likes real."

Gertrude rocked gently in her wheelchair. "I'm still not quite sure how to pronounce your first name." She touched her ear. "My hearing."

"Oh, I'm so sorry. In North America people call me Joe. Much easier, yes?"

"I like that – and you must call me Gertrude. By the way – your English – you sound so American."

"Aw, good reason for that. My mother made it possible for me to go to UCLA when I was seventeen for arts, drama and movies. You see now? That's why I'm in the business."

Gertrude pushed the box of Ganong's again. Joisie's deft fingers plucked another.

"You're very close to your mother, aren't you, Joe."

He finished savouring his chocolate. "Yes, very close. Without her, I'm nothing. You see, I have four older brothers." He shook his head, the ready smile gone. "When I was a boy, they beat me. My father did nothing. Only my mother protected me."

Gertrude rocked forward. "That's so sad. Why on earth would they do that?"

"I'm different. They knew that. So did my father."

"Different, Joe? How so?"

Joe looked up earnestly, pressing his fists into the chest of his suit. "You have a saying – in the closet?"

Gertrude softly rocked back. "But, Joe, surely your family accepts you these days."

He smiled again, softening, and hands folded in his lap. "Yakushita – it's a big company. You know that."

"I do."

"I'm a member of the board, but I never attend. They don't want me. Only my mother always understood me. I was crazy about

27

all kinds of movies, even as a little boy. When she decided that it was best for me to leave home and go to UCLA, I was reborn. I graduated, went to work for Advent Studios, just a low-level job, but it was a dream come true. I was in Hollywood and working in the movies, but I always went home to see my mother and tell her everything."

Joe sat up and pointed a finger. "Now, here is what happened. My mother is a great power in Yakushita. She doesn't sit on the board, but owns many shares. My brothers, my father, everybody – they all fear her. Behind her back, they call her the witch. She doesn't care. So, when I was twenty-four I went home for my birthday. Little did I know that my mother had been buying up shares in Advent Studios and now she had controlling interest. So, what does she give me for my birthday? She makes me the new CEO of Advent Studios."

"My goodness. So, it's your mother who owns Advent Studios."

Joisei clasped his hands, a warm smile on his pale gold face. He chuckled before he spoke. "In name only. I am always the boss."

***

The morning was gone and they had eaten the BLT sandwiches. The Patterson printing plant had a cafeteria and it was easy to order them over, along with cookies and coffee. Now Joisei Yakushita dabbed his mouth with a napkin. He still smiled affably, dark eyes friendly.

"Advent has a contract with you for the third Zenith, the trilogy book. When can I have it?" he said softly, even innocently.

Gertrude Bachalder pushed the Ganong chocolate box over. She too smiled calmly.

They'd already eaten through the first layer, Joisei studied the bottom chocolates.

"Ah, I love the cherries," he said.

"You're welcome to the third Zenith, Joe, after you pay me what you owe me." She had selected a soft centre and now she finished it off.

Joisei chuckled. "We come to that, eh? So, how much do you think I owe you?"

"Forensic accounting says eight million, but of course the Los Angeles court will probably award twice that."

If Joisei was startled by this figure, he didn't show it. He folded his hands in his lap.

"When I was seventeen years old, I saw my first Zenith movie." He shook his head slowly. "Even then I saw that the production was not so good. The second Zenith, not much better. It's no wonder it did so poorly in the USA, but much better everywhere else." Now he nodded. "Even then I knew I could do better – much better. And now I'm ready to do it. I have the capital; my Hong Kong martial art movies provided that." He lifted his hands. "I believe in Zenith: the story line is straightforward, progressive, almost like a John Ford western. Too bad I can't have John Wayne, eh?"

Gertrude's wheelchair gently rocked, making its own music. "But first you must pay me, Joe."

Joisei warm smile could be most disarming. He shrugged and opened his hands. "My mother owns a lot of property, and yes, there are occasions when something has to be settled in court, but for her that is definitely a last resource." He shook his head. "I do not like the court solution either." His arms went out wide and he practically stood up. "Yes, I have come a long way to see you." He relaxed back in his seat, his open hands up, making an appealing gesture. "This is the Yakushita way: when the time is right, you move directly toward an obstacle and make the necessary changes so it is not so much of a problem anymore."

"Ah, I see," Gertrude said. "So, I am the obstacle."

He shook his head, "No, no, I don't say that. But the fact is – you ask too much."

"I only ask what you owe me, Joe." She put a hand up and stroked her chin. "I like the Yakushita way. We could settle this right now. I'll take two million off."

"Off what?"

"Off the sixteen million of course."

He chuckled, eyes crinkling at the corners and shook his head. "Oh, come now, you can do better than that."

"So can you. What's your best offer?"

"So, you throw it back on me, eh?" he said laughing. "Okay, why don't we do this?" He took out a pen and business card. Joisei placed the card on the desk and tapped a finger on it. "Ah, dear Gertrude, what shall we do with you?" He stared up at the ceiling like he was pondering, but not for long. He scribbled on the card and pushed it across the desk.

Gertrude read it. Eight million. Tops. She took a desk pen, crossed it off and wrote under it. Twelve million or we go to LA court. She pushed the card back.

Joisei glanced at it and smiled with his whole face again. "I don't think my mother would like you very much."

"Maybe not."

Joisei placed his hands flat on the desk, his face serious now. "Would you say publishing fiction is a gamble?"

Gertrude shrugged. "Absolutely. Most fiction does not make money."

Joisei sat back and opened his hands again. "Not so with me. Almost all my movies have made money." He put his hands in his lap and leaned forward, nodding his head. "It's definitely going to cost me more money but I'd be willing to go partners and let you have points in the new Zenith production." He nodded again for emphasis. "I am a modern movie maker, so I'll be using all the latest technology. I intend Zenith to be a big international movie." He sat back and waited for her response.

Gertrude patted down her wavy, platinum hair. The last of the eastern sun was at the window and making her round glasses sparkle. At last she smiled and put her hands together.

"It's the old saying, Jose, a bird in hand is better than two in the bush."

Joisei laughed. "It's uncanny, that is one of my mother's favorite sayings, but you may regret it when you see what I'm going to create."

It was Gertrude's turn to laugh. "No I won't. Our contract with Advent Studios calls for three Zenith books – and it does provide points in the movie productions. No, Joisei, what we're talking here is what you owe me. Let's settle up. Make me a decent offer so that we don't have to end up in an LA court. You say your mother doesn't like that and neither do I."

Joisei's smile lessened but was still friendly. They sat silently for a while considering each other. Finally, Joisei spoke.

"I'll give you ten million."

Now Gertrude smiled broadly. "I can't get up – you'll have to come around here and we'll shake on it."

Chapter 10

Roger, Harry's Gaylord lawyer, had waited almost five minutes for Harry to make it to the phone. It was 10 a.m., so the lawyer figured Harry might be up, even though he knew that Harry was very ill and probably dying, but this was an important phone call, probably the most important for Harry in the past ten years.

"Hello, Harry? I didn't want to bother you but …"

"That's okay, Roger, what's up?" Harry's voice was now coarse and dark after his long illness.

"You're not going to believe this, Harry, but I think the ice jam has finally broken up." The lawyer's voice still held disbelief. "What's it been? Ten years of litigation? And now finally. Are you sitting down, Harry?"

There was a pause … "Harry? You're still there?"

Finally, "Yeah, I'm still here, Roger. But you got me baffled … the ice jam has broken?"

"Hold on to your hat, Harry. I've just had this incredible talk with Patterson Printing's legal people. Yakushita has had people in Collingwood for the past three days. It seems they're bypassing Advent's legal team and settling this whole thing face to face with Patterson. They're still there, and now I need some advice from you. You're the last piece of the puzzle, Harry."

Another silence, although Roger could hear Harry's raspy breathing.

"All this has happened without me? Oh yeah, I forgot, I'm only the author." Another pause.

"Harry?"

"Yeah, I'm here. Does this mean I might get some money?"

"I told you to hang on to your hat. This could mean that you'll be back in business. Probably better off than ever. You just have to agree to a few things."

"Oh, oh. Those old few things, eh?"

"Here's the ticket. Yakushita apparently bought Advent Film works ten years ago for only one reason: they wanted control of the Zenith movies. That's why they practically shut Advent down afterwards. They had what they wanted: Zenith. Are you with me so far, Harry?"

"Sure. Why else would Yakushita buy a small Indie movie company? But why did they screw me and Patterson Printing? Advent wasn't broke, after all."

"They almost totally froze Advent's assets. The Zenith income stream they mostly kept for themselves. So, by now Advent has probably cost them nothing."

"Yeah, my money."

"True, but now it looks like we've got a solution, Harry. Are you ready for this?"

"Jesus, just go ahead and tell me, Roger."

"First of all, they know there's another Zenith book so they want to buy it. It's incredible. These guys want Advent to make another Zenith movie. Yakushita's got the dough, Harry."

Harry had a coughing spasm.

"You okay, Harry?"

"Listen, Roger, these assholes owe me a bundle. I've been paid hardly anything for Zenith in more than five years. What are they going to do about that? I seem to be doing a little dying these days, so this whole thing is getting boring."

"I know, Harry," Roger said contritely. "It's been dreadful, but listen to this. Patterson wants to take a settlement. The forensic audit showed over eight millions dollars owing. It's probably a helluva lot more than that. It seems Patterson has already has a tentative settlement with Yakushita. And a little birdie tells me that Patterson wants to give you around three million. Is that going to work?"

Another pause. "I ain't accepting the first offer, Roger. I never have, dying or not. Let's ask for four and then take three and a half."

Roger laughed, "Just what I was going suggest. Now that leaves the new Zenith project. Patterson has accepted a tentative deal there, too. They won't say what, but they want to give you two hundred thousand up front and the rest based on your old agency. Can you accept that?"

"Jesus!" Harry wheezed, "This talk of money is making me dizzy. Tell them I want three hundred thousand and settle for two hundred and fifty. The agency deal is fine. Patterson has always been fair to me."

"I hear you, Harry. There's a settlement along these lines for sure. How does it feel to be well off again?"

"That depends. Right now, I'm broke, Roger. Our friend Gerry at the TD Bank wants to foreclose on my house. When can I see some real green here?"

"That could take some time, Harry, probably as much as three months. But listen, under these new circumstances, with your permission, I could talk to Gerry, even give him a letter of understanding, that sort of thing. Soon you'll have lots of money and a golden income stream so I'm sure Gerry will be happy."

"Great. I need to keep the roof over my head."

"Don't worry," Roger laughed. "You're back to favourite son status. Just get well enough to be at our next poker game."

Chapter 11

A tall young woman was standing in the portico of Moxley Towers, only it wasn't much of a tower being merely three stories, still it was a condo building for the upper middle class of Gaylord. It was just past noon on a Friday and fluffy snow was falling on this chilly mid-December day. She bent to a pedestal that had sand in it and butted out a cigarette, then turned to watch a hefty woman head up the recently brushed sidewalk. She had on a white toque above her dark sunglasses and was wearing an ordinary knee-length blue parka against the below zero chill. She toted a fully laden shopping bag, probably groceries, and a brown paper bag clutched to her chest, probably booze. The two met at the entrance.

The girl pushed her sunglasses to the top of her silver blonde hair.

"I'll bet anything you're Alva," she said with a broad disarming smile.

The lady was taken aback, stopped in her tracks. She was easily middle-aged, and wide in her blue parka. "Hello?" she said questionably.

"I'm Moxxanne. I left a message on your answering machine?"

The lady took a couple of steps closer to her foyer entrance before pausing. "Oh, you're the one. Look, whatever you're selling I don't want any."

The girl stepped up to the foyer and was more than a few inches taller than the woman. "I'm not selling anything. I just want to talk to you about Gaylord and Harry."

The lady put her heavy bag down so she could open the foyer door and then looked sternly over her shoulder. "What for?"

"I met a lady at your library where I was doing research and she told me you might be a good person to talk to, so I looked up your number and left you a message, but you didn't return my call."

The lady put her sunglasses on top of her toque. She had dark eyes in a pale aging face. "What woman told you that?" she said curtly.

The girl shrugged but still smiled brightly. "Just a lady. She said she once worked for you at your pharmacy."

"Oh for God's sake," the woman said. "It's that goddamned Verda – I might have known." Her plain lips showed exasperation. "Well, grab that bag and step inside here for a moment."

The foyer was a welcome place from the frosty outside. They both stamped their boots. The woman still clutched her bag of booze.

"So what's this got to do with Gaylord and Harry? And who the hell are you?"

The girl put the grocery bag down. She was surprised at how heavy it was and wondered how far the woman had lugged it. "I told you my name – Moxxanne. I'm from Ryerson University and I'm here doing research for a project we're doing."

The woman carefully put her booze bag down and pulled off her mittens. "What kind of project?"

"We started it a couple of years ago. I was just a cub reporter and we did this essay on Harry. It was sponsored by our Arts and Theatre faculty and it just kind of surprised everybody because it created a lot of interest that nobody expected, so that's why I'm here. I'm just doing investigative reporting, that's all."

The woman frowned, a lived in face but with character and faded beauty. "You don't say." Her dark eyes brimmed with suspicion. "So what are you taking at Ryerson?"

Moxxanne's face shone with youthful beauty. "Didn't I say on my phone message? Sorry – I'm in law – third year."

The frown deepened.

"Law, eh. And you wouldn't also happen to be working for a law firm?" She shoved her key into the lock but didn't turn it.

Moxxanne face still beamed. "I'm third year and not articling. This is strictly research for our story. Look, I'd be happy to give you my editor's phone number if you want?"

Alva pulled the heavy security door open and then moved her bags inside. "That won't be necessary."

She half stepped through the door. "I still don't see what you're after."

Moxxanne stepped close but didn't put her hand on the door. "We're just trying to find out why Harry's such a mystery, even here in Gaylord."

Alva pulled the door so it was nearly closed. "Look, this is all very nice and good luck, but I am just not interested." She pulled the door shut and there was a solid click as the lock set.

If Moxxanne was put off she didn't show it, she strolled leisurely down the walk. The cold didn't seem to bother her even though she was puffing frosty breath. Her Ford Mustang rental was just down the street. Once in the car she took out a small recording device and began making observations on her meeting with Alva.

Chapter 12

The Eagle's Club was mostly a plain Jane affair, a tap room with a five stool bar, a small stage with piano, a mini dance floor and twelve tables with chairs. There was a table off the bar in a corner that was larger, and afforded some privacy for small meetings and so forth. There were no windows but it was well lit for the few late afternoon members. At the larger table sat Orson and Moxxanne. She had just narrowly defeated him at the snooker table in the adjoining games room. They both had draft beers and bags of potato chips in front of them.

"You played this game before, Moxxanne. I play often and I win more than I lose. Mind you, that wasn't my A-game. I only got serious when I saw you could play."

The girl brushed a flank of silver blonde hair from her pale face and light eyes. "Whaddya think we do at Ryerson? Just books? Bring your A-game. Maybe I'll win again."

Her smile was fetching and showed off her pretty face – the kind that was sort of old Greek – an attic artiste might go for it.

"Oh, we'll play again," Orson said over his glass. "I'm not done with you by a long shot, young lady." He, too, had light eyes but they were narrow, almost beady but still lively and mischievous. His fringe of white hair was noosed at the back.

Moxxanne was munching up her chips and had drained the beer. She was tall and healthy looking and with a youthful edgy voice. "By the way, at Tim Hortons I knew you weren't my Uncle Harry."

"Oh yeah? Well he ain't nowhere near as good looking as me. I suppose you've seen pictures of 'im, eh?"

Her blue blouse flaunted cleavage. "I did a paper on Uncle Harry for Ryerson two years ago. I bet I know more about him than you do."

Orson leaned back, the small eyes merry and he stabbed the air with a forefinger. It was a boxer's hand, heavy and stubby fingered." Oh you think you do, eh?" It was mid-December and freezing outside but he was wearing his usual white t-shirt, short sleeves rolled so they showed his old boxer muscles. "We're both from Gaylord, only he's much older than I am."

"Much older? Careful. I know his birth date."

"Don't be cheeky – five years older."

She took a thirsty swallow of fresh beer. "So, that makes you seventy."

Orson waggled the finger again, "Don't be saucy. I'm not seventy. Not 'til next September."

Moxxanne laughed. "So what's up with you and Uncle Harry? Your his valet or something?"

Orson's lips drooped, an exaggerated hurt look. "If that was the case Harry would be my valet. I'm his best friend, and his guardian angel. Without me, you wouldn't have no Uncle Harry. I practically invented him."

Moxxanne was momentarily stopped, eyes blinking slowly. "Then how is it I don't know much about you from my research papers?"

Orson plucked a napkin from the chromium canister and dabbed his lips. He shrugged, "Why should you? I'm not a writer. I'm a blue collar guy who has been Harry's best friend for forty years. I'm not in the limelight."

"But you say you invented him."

Orson swigged beer and then dabbed at his lips again. "Sure I did. That first novel of his? The Relentless Gun? Without me that wouldn't have happened. See, everything started from that. And that was forty years ago."

When Moxxanne smiled it was like neon in her pale face. "I know Harry's work. The CBC made an hour long TV show out of that book back in the early seventies. It had fair ratings. And you say you started that?"

Orson had natural aplomb. When you handed him something he rode with it. "Absolutely. It was me that spotted that Patterson Printing Company's poster at our library. 'Well, would you look at that?' I thought. 'A contest for new Canadian writers – and the winner would get published.' And here was Harry with his first novel, except he wasn't doing a damn thing with it, just letting it lay around gathering dust. You see, Harry didn't have any confidence in himself, didn't think the book was good enough and flat out refused to enter the contest. So I grabbed the manuscript and took it to a friend at the library and she took care of boxing it up and all that. So naturally she asks me – what's the title? – because it didn't have one, but I knew Harry was using this working title – The Relentless Gun. And no doubt you know what happened after that. Shit, they should put up a plaque in Gaylord Library for me kicking off Harry's career like that. How's that for something a friend would do?"

Orson clasped his knotty arms behind his head, the arms and chest hair matching his white fringe. "Aw, I've been moving him around like a chess piece for years. I practically potty trained him, changed his nappy and sprinkled talcum on his arse."

"You invented Uncle Harry? How so?"

Orson's arms came down, elbows on the table. "I taught him everything he knows from girls to golf balls. Y'see, he's your typical imagination kind of guy. Sitting down – smart as hell – standing up – dumb as duck shit. I used to meet guys like that in the boxing ring. Couldn't hardly find their way out of their own corners. I clobbered 'em."

It was Moxxanne's turn to point a finger.

"Ah ha! Popeye! I bet you were good."

Orson shrugged modestly. "I don't have cauliflower ears."

"Yeah, but you got a pug nose, and your face is all punched smooth."

Orson put his hands to his face and peeked through his fingers. "My girlfriends don't mind. They think I'm cute."

"When did you first meet Uncle Harry?"

"You doin' research now?"

"Maybe."

"Okay," he touched his jaw. "Hell, I dunno, I guess it was at the Rolling Mills – the steel plant we've got here. We kind of buddied up and I took 'im under my wing. We were like thirty and thirty-five years old, something like that. I had finished my boxing and had gone back to the mill. We were both single, and fancy free if you know what I mean."

"Fancy free – I love that. That's what I am – fancy free."

"I'll bet you are."

"So what happened after that? You both lived happily ever after?"

Orson took a long swig and licked his lips.

"Something like that. Life is farce … punctuated by tragedy."

"Hoo," Moxxanne rolled her eyes. "Now you're sounding like the writer."

Orson shook his head. "Naw, but I've always been a better reader than Harry. I've always loved libraries."

"Me too. That's why I went to work at Patterson's. Lotsa books."

Orson stared at her and then put his glass down with a clunk. "Did I hear you right? You worked at Patterson's?"

Moxxanne opened her hands innocently. "Of course. I am from Collingwood after all."

Orson stared stupidly and then shook his head. "Wait a god-damned minute. You at Patterson's? This is a coincidence?"

Moxxanne shrugged. "No coincidence – my mother's a Patterson editor."

Orson sat back and clapped his hands to his ears. "Holy shit. Harry was right. You are trouble – big trouble."

Moxxanne gave her silver locks a shake and put her hands to her chest. "Me trouble? How's that?"

Orson's face had soured, no more smile. "If you are who you say you are, then you must know that Harry and Patterson's are both involved in a big legal fight. This whole mess has bankrupted Harry, and probably ruined his health, and if you know that – then what the hell are you doing in Gaylord?" Orson pointed an accusatory finger. "You're a law student. Who the hell are you working for?"

Moxxanne brushed at silver hair, eyes calm, innocent. "I worked for Patterson Printing when I was a teenager. Why wouldn't I? My mother, Della Lolly, is lead editor at Patterson's. First I worked in the book-binding and printing plant, and then my mother moved me over to the publishing house. I told you, I love books. That's where I got to read most of Harry's stuff."

Orson waved his hands like he was trying to brush away an imaginary cobweb. "Jesus, they do say truth is stranger than fiction." Orson calmed, laying his hands on the table. "I can't believe it … Della Lolly … editor on Harry's Zenith books … and she's your mother?"

Moxxanne smiled, "Right, my mother."

Orson nodded. "I'm slow but I'll get there. Tell me again, why do you say you're Harry's niece?"

Moxxanne clasped her fingers. "My mother has always claimed that it was Early. That's what she claims and that's all I know – so far."

Orson passed his hands over his bald pate, like he was smooth-ing down imaginary hair. "So this Early – he's Harry's brother?"

"No, silly, that would be my grandfather. My mother claims that Early Jr. is my father."

Orson face wasn't so smooth anymore, it twisted up. "Okay, my mistake. Early Jr. is your father. Right?"

"That's what my mother claims."

"Claims? What's this claims?"

Moxxanne was all innocence. "Early and my mother were at Ryerson together. Good friends, that's all. Then my mother got to be thirty-three years old, no husband, no children. So she called her good friend Early Jr. and got him to donate sperm. She wanted a child – just a child – no husband. So you see? I'm a tube baby."

Orson was silent, head nodding slowly. Finally he said, "But you can't quite get around to accepting it."

It was Moxxanne's time to be silent. Finally she spoke, "Maybe I do, maybe I don't."

Orson's hands were back on the table. "Does this have something to do with why you're in Gaylord? You're searching? And not sure you even know what for?"

"Oh, I have an idea – maybe you can help me."

"How's that?"

"How well did Harry know my mother?"

Orson sat up. "What's Harry got to do with it?"

"Harry spent time in Collingwood for his Zenith books, and my mother was lead editor. And that was before I was born."

Orson put his hands on his cheeks. "So. I see. It's Harry, eh? But if that's true, why would your mother let him off the hook?"

Moxxanne flicked silver strands from her face. "Aw, even as a kid, I never quite believed my mother's story about Early Jr. and his gift of daddy sperm. She was telling me something but her face was saying something else. Kids pick up on that."

"So what's all this about Harry?"

"I was a snoop. I found letters – oh, they were innocent enough – but they did prove that my mother and Harry were close. But their letters didn't tell me what I wanted to know."

"About what?"

"That maybe I'm not a sperm baby after all, maybe I'm more of a love child. I think my mother and Harry might have done a deal – a weekend stand. Not love, but maybe as close as either one of them could get to it."

She waited while Orson rubbed his hands. "So you've come to Gaylord to find out the truth about Harry. But you're running out of time."

"Maybe so. But you'll help me get to see Harry, won't you, Orson?"

Orson continued to rub his hands. "Maybe," he said at last.

Chapter 13

Moxxanne was an impulsive person so as soon as she passed the cop car parked at the curb she knew what she was going to do. They were on Main Street at the edge of town going south toward Winnipeg. She'd tested out her rented Mustang, so she knew it was easy to break the rear tires free and raise a ruckus.

It was a cold mid-December day, easily twenty below, but the sun was shining and the pavement was dry. Time: 2:00 p.m. At fifty feet past the cop car, she punched the Mustang, chirped the rear tires, and caused the end to step out. Then she braked hard and ran it to the curb, cut the motor, and punched up the four way flashers, all the time watching the cop in the rear view mirror. She definitely had his attention.

The Crown Vic came to life, but with no siren or flashing lights. It just crept up the hundred and fifty feet that was between them and came to a stop. A tall lanky cop stepped out and then reached back to fetch his cap. He stopped at her left tail light and eyeballed the situation. Moxxanne raised her right hand where he could see it and gave him a friendly finger wave. He stepped to her door where the window was already down. He bent over to get a good look at her, and was caught by a merciless smile that took no prisoners.

The tall officer was resistant, at least so far. The sunglasses were black and his face unsmiling he was younger, hardly thirty.

"What was that all about?" he said, police officer all the way.

"Oh thank you so much," Moxxanne said leaning to the window.

The cop caught the perfume and straightened up like he was about to be asphyxiated.

"Thanks for what?" he said.

"You saved me a trip so thank you so much," Moxxanne said, a sexy scratchy voice.

The cop had his hands in his police parka pockets now, against the chill. He bent and rechecked the rear seat. He straightened.

Moxxanne's head was partly out the window, she looked up at him, showing her whole radiant face.

"I thought I'd have to go to the police station," she said as though this was already a big relief.

He bent again, partly to get out of the icy northeast wind so that their heads were only a foot apart.

"Whaddya wanna go there for?" The perfume got him this time, a good whiff of it.

She laughed as if it were all very silly, hands outspread. She was wearing fingerless gloves to go with her black biker jacket.

"It's on my list, Officer – it definitely says talk to a police officer." She put her right hand out the window and tapped her watch. She was left handed. "Surely you guys are entitled to a break at three o'clock? There's a Tim Hortons back there and I'd love to treat you to something hot, it's so freezing out."

The cop snapped straight again and looked around like maybe somebody was watching and listening. "I don't know if I could do that," he said.

Moxxanne's face became beseechingly innocent and her fingers came in and touched her chest. "Oh, I'm not trying to pull a funny one, Officer, but I can see how you might have thought that. I know you guys can't be too careful. No, I'm on the level – I just want to buy that coffee and hopefully catch a tiny bit of advice from you. That would be all right, wouldn't it?"

He looked around again, stalling. Where was the catch?

"As soon as I see you at Timmies, I'm gonna put my ID and my car rental papers right in front of you. You'll want to see them, right?"

He still didn't smile, his square jaw firm, but he nodded, like this last part was his idea.

Moxxanne put her gloved hand out, like she was collecting her spoils. "My name's Moxxanne. What's yours?"

He took her hand. "Ray," he said, and even offered his last name. "Ray Nolan."

"See ya at Tim's," she said, the big grabby smile again. Moxxanne took off slowly, made an illegal U-turn right in front of him and headed back towards Tim Hortons.

Chapter 14

Moxxanne's weight was around one thirty-eight and at five feet nine she was now using all of it. If her hips were any wider they wouldn't have been just about perfect. Officer Ray Nolan was under her and he was just getting the coup de grâce. She could see by his face that he was just about done for.

Moxxanne had settled into Burner's Motel on December 15, two days ago. It fit into the bare-bones budget she was on, located just on the outskirts of Gaylord and therefore handy to everything. It was the kind of place that every town has, where horny townies go to get their rocks off and where travellers would still find the place more or less up to snuff.

She was out of the bathroom, a towel coifed around her head and wearing a shorty kimono. She plopped on a chair, legs parted so that her red nest showed – nothing shaven – a natural woman. Officer Ray Nolan had already been to the can and was now hustling himself into his cop gear. She could tell by his face that he was already suffering adulterer's remorse – a thirty-year-old man, married and with five-year-old twin daughters – he'd never been off the garden path – until now. Dressed, he sat on the bed, bent and put his head in his hands.

Moxxanne's green eyes went over him, absorbing his body language. She was slowly masticating a new pink slug of bubble gum, savouring its tingly sugar bite. She got up and sat beside the crestfallen Ray – a mother beside a son. She ran her hand comfortingly back and forth across his furry, brown brush cut.

"You're a good looking guy, Ray," she said softly. "Tall, well built, and then there's the uniform. What you gotta understand is that makes you just like catnip to women. So, see, none of this is your fault."

She blew a bubble but didn't pop it, just sucked it soundlessly back in. She moved her hand down and rubbed his back, up and down, up and down. Slowly she felt his tension easing away.

"So you're going to help me with that stuff we were talking about at Hortons aren't you, Ray," she said matter-of-factly.

He straightened, rubbing the back of his hands against his cheeks, as if tears might have actually fallen.

"I said I'd try. I don't know if we have anything on Harry going back as far you want."

She continued to rub.

"That's okay. Like I said, I just want to confirm that Harry was more or less a normal Gaylord teenager."

Ray Nolan was driving back towards the Gaylord police station, "Goddamn," he was thinking over and over, "I've been fucking compromised."

He kept shaking his head ruefully. "Sonofabitch. I've been fucking compromised."

He did not know, nor would he ever know, how she had managed to do this to him.

Chapter 15

It was getting late December now in Gaylord, snow massed against every standing thing in this cold winter, the poor bare trees, except for the firs, shivering in Harry's yard, and a dull sun just past high noon. As usual these days, Harry had taken a little lunch and sat hunched behind his old-fashioned hardwood desk. Not long ago, Harry stood six foot one and weighed about one eighty-five; a lanky but hardy cowboy of a man who had survived a number of motor-cycle tumbles as well as a few turnover car wrecks. But now, he was sunken-chested, spavined and gaunt-faced behind the desk. For in only the past two years of his present seventy-five he had become sorely decrepitated.

His shaggy white hair, sparsely shot with black, hung down his furrowed brow, but his dark eyes, although decidedly beady, remained observant. Stubborn even unto his present debilitating illness, a Cristo cigar was clenched in his yellowed teeth and his claw of a hand was wrapped around a glass containing three fingers of Gentleman Jack bourbon. He brushed the cowlick of hair off his bushy, old man's eyebrows.

"So, Orson, what have you found out about your snoopy student?" His voice was coarse with age but on this day clear.

"I've been working on it," Orson said, his right hand on a bottle of Coors Light.

Orson's soft chair was just off to the right of Harry, closer to the fieldstone fireplace, which had not seen fire in many years but was still part of the many amenities in Harry's not quite big enough to be a mansion home. They were on the upstairs floor in Harry's den or writing room as he liked to call it, though it had it once served as the master bedroom in the original layout of the house.

"She really is a law student from Ryerson, doing background for a story on you. That part is legit." Although five years younger, at seventy, Orson could easily be taken for a younger man, having still not lost his pugnacious physical presence. He was wearing his usual, for both winter and summer, black biker's jacket with its attendant buckle. He was hairless save for a grey fringe around the ears, the eyes sternly green and riveting, a compelling part of his face. He was amazingly wrinkle free, possibly having been punched perpetually smooth from his early professional boxing career, which was further marked off by a pug nose. He did have a double chin as a giveaway to his true age.

Harry sipped his whiskey, shaky hand and all, but did not spill.

"Harmless then. Make sure you keep her the hell away from me."

Orson set his bottle on the desk blotter.

"I'm not sure that's gonna be possible, Harry. Like I told you before, you're gonna want to meet her." Orson decided not to remind Harry of their earlier conversation. He'd just gotten out of the hospital, was on medication and drinking whiskey that day.

Harry's slit eyes were testy.

"What the hell are you talking about? You said she was just the usual nosy student. Why the hell would I want to meet her?"

Orson leaned forward, an elbow on the desk, "First of all, she's bloody good looking, Harry. Think of a young Kim Basinger. Just breathing this kid in will do you good." He tapped his bottle on the desk for emphasis.

Harry shook his head, "Aw for chrissake, Orson. I'm past that shit."

"Maybe so," Orson persisted, "but there's something else I gotta tell you about her."

Harry studied Orson's face, he knew the man only too well.

"This is not on me," Orson said decidedly. "This is on you. That's why you should probably see her, I mean even if your health is not so good these days."

Harry was still in his fuzzy, white bathrobe; he seemed seldom out of it these days. Now he sank into it pulling it close around his bony shoulders as though it would hold off the world.

"That's putting it mildly," he said ruefully. "I'm at death's door for chrissake."

Orson shook his head as much as his thick neck would allow. "Aw shit, Harry, I hate to hear you talk this way. Now you listen here. This Moxxanne girl is related to you. I just got more details from her last night."

Harry put his cigar in the big ashtray. "Related? How the fuck could that be?"

"I know, I know, it's weird, but she let something slip last night and by this morning I figured it out."

Harry's face clenched, "Last night? Where were you? Your trailer?"

Orson stiffened, "Oh for chrissake, Harry. Yes, we were at the trailer. But it wasn't like that. She drank four of my Coors and then buggered off. She might be a young chick but she can drink like a man. Didn't seem to fizz on her. She told me about how she grew up in Collingwood, Ontario. Yeah, that's right, same town as your publisher, Patterson Printing. Am I getting your attention now?"

Harry stretched up out of his robe and brushed hair out of his eyes. "So maybe this isn't so innocent after all. What else do you know?"

Orson pushed back on the soft chair, beer in hand. "As a teenager she worked for Patterson Printing, and lo and behold they had all these books on you. She's a very smart kid. Didn't take her long to put it all together after that."

"Put what together?"

"That she's related to you."

Lately Harry became upset easily and now his thin voice rose. "Quit fucking around, Orson. She can't be related to me. You of all people should know that."

Orson smiled. "I do. I asked a lot of questions about her background, parents and so forth. She gave straight answers. She was raised by her mother in Collingwood. The father? Now get this – she claims she's the result of a sperm donation. So, she never really had a father. But here's the thing. The guy that donated the sperm? His name was Early. Yeah, that's right, the same as your brother."

Harry rocked back on the swivel chair, bony hands clasping, eyes up and down. "Unlikely – Early is seventy-two years old." He rocked some more. "But his son, also named Early, well, he could be the guy. He's got some kind of reputation that bird."

"That's what I was thinking, and that would make you kinda like an uncle, right?"

Harry shook his head. "I don't get it. Is she going to use this as some kind of bargaining chip?"

Orson drained his Coors and wiped his mouth with the back of his hand. "I think she planned on using it to get an audience with you, but then she found out you weren't doing so good health-wise, so she told me she doesn't have to meet with you, not if I help her with her background search."

Harry managed an ironic grin. "Good old Orson, taking the fall for me again." He rubbed his knuckles across a chin that needed a shave. "Let's find out if her old man really is my black sheep nephew." His chair made a creaking noise as the wheels came forward.

"I'll call up my brother. Maybe he knows about it."

Orson frowned. "Jesus, you two talking again?"

Harry tilted his head. "Depends. It's a brother thing. He's up there in Dauphin running his auto empire and I'm down here in Gaylord trying to sell books. We're oil and water, always have been. I'm not mad at him, it's just awkward, that's all."

Orson chuckled. "What are you going to ask him? Did your son Early jerk off in a bottle for some dame in Collingwood twenty-three years ago?"

Harry put his head back against the tall chair and rubbed his hands into dry eye sockets. "We gotta know if it's the right Early. That's something we gotta know."

Chapter 16

Harry woke up, four o'clock in the morning, the usual cold sweat, the terrible dread, the horror, the Nitehawk dream again, the same one over and over, the whole thing so damn vivid, down to the particular burnt-peanut smell in the cockpit. Of course, he didn't mind the part where he was cruising serenely over Gaylord at three thousand feet in the already dark mid-December sky, the frog belly gleam of instruments all correct and satisfying. He had the Nitehawk computer "note pad" open to the "SHUT DOWN AND RESTART ENGINES" procedure.

There is always a certain trepidation when a pilot deliberately shuts down perfectly serviceable engines – it goes against one's ingrained common sense – but shut them down he did. The mini turbo props were quiet anyway and there was always the airborne wind noise so the dead engines seemed to make little difference. He counted off the test required ten seconds and tapped the appropriate switches.

Nothing.

Harry was an amateur pilot but probably a pretty good one, especially with the Nitehawk, which he had fallen in love with when he had co-piloted it back to Gaylord almost five years ago. It was not a popular aircraft with the co-op members, too technically new and twitchy for pleasure pilots, but Harry and a few other pilots liked it for those very reasons.

Harry was generally a calm person but the Nitehawk was not a good glide aircraft and now it was demanding he do something. He reworked the restart procedure from the beginning, five steps in all, and clicked the START ENGINE buttons again. Nothing.

The Nitehawk began to fall out of the sky.

He twisted the Nitehawk's glide so that it would make circles and keep him over the airfield. He had automatically made his emergency report and the responses starting going back and forth, but the Nitehawk didn't like the darkened sky anymore and was starting to pull, at first just a tug, and then the fight was on. The wind noise rose steadily, almost a shriek now. Harry was taking the down side of a roller coaster ride as he steadily fell upon the small city of Gaylord.

Pilots generally say they remember little about the final moments in an air struggle for life and death. Harry saw the steeple of a Gaylord church immediately rushing up to him – absolutely no way to miss it – but he did. Then the trees, a line of them, there was a huge swoosh, like a brush had touched him, and then there was the highway. The Nitehawk was coming in for a landing, seemingly all by itself. Instinctively Harry moved to drop the wheels – there was no power so it shouldn't happen – still, he felt the familiar "ka-chunk" as the wheels came down.

It felt just like a normal runway landing, the same jolt up through the spine on touchdown, and squeaking rasp of the tires, only he was heading straight down the middle of a Gaylord public thoroughfare, several cars dodging off the road in front of him.

And then they were stopped – right in front of the Gaylord Civic Hospital – and to Harry's astonishment, the Nitehawk's engines were running. He found he was still able to speak to the tower, relaying his situation. And he felt calm, too calm, for all of a sudden his hands, his feet, his whole body was beginning to quiver.

Soon police cruisers arrived and took up positions in front and behind the Nitehawk, blocking all traffic. Amazingly, no car accident had occurred and no one hurt. Paramedics arrived. Two firetrucks. It took a while to get Harry out of the aircraft – shock had set in and he was practically frozen stiff.

Chapter 17

Roger had been watching over the rim of his Tim Hortons coffee mug from his corner seat where he could see both doors, and now he saw a tall blonde girl step through the front one, and watched her stamp the snow off her boots on the mat as her eyes went around the shop and landed on him. He saw the mutual recognition and she headed over.

They didn't speak, just a nod back and forth while she shrugged off her bike jacket, plopped it on an empty chair along with her satchel sized purse. Once seated and directly across from him, Roger saw that she was attractive: long, wavy, straw hair, cool green eyes, an assured, ready smile.

She extended a hand. "Thanks for seeing me like this, Roger. You must be a busy guy."

Roger accepted her long fingered but firm hand shake and studied her face, years of lawyering had made him a keen judge of first meetings. He nodded, satisfied and released her hand. "Did you say your name was, ah, Roxanne?"

She pushed blonde waves back from her face, smile brightening. "Actually, it's Moxxanne, two X's, but don't worry, people do that all the time – I kind of enjoy it."

"I see," Roger said. He was a large man, three hundred pounds with a small pursed mouth, head like a basketball, greyish silver wavelets of hair combed straight back and a neck that was scarcely discernible. His voice was soft for such a large fellow. A navy blazer barely managed to encase the humpty-dumpty belly and displayed an attractive, striped, matching tie. He was meticulously shaven, eyes keen and narrow under greying brows. He looked his part, an older, senior-partner lawyer. He cupped soft looking hands. "Well, young lady, I'm not quite sure what it is that you want from me."

"Right now, a latte, but I can get it myself. Do you mind?"

Roger shrugged, obviously miffed, "Oh, all right. But see here, I only have twenty minutes."

Moxxanne returned, took a sip and dabbed her red lips with the napkin. "I know you can't tell me confidential stuff about Harry but that's not what I'm looking for."

Roger's small mouth made a frown. "Of course I can't. You say you're taking law at Ryerson?"

"That's right, third year."

"What field of law?"

"Criminal."

The big head tipped slightly, lips almost a sneer. "Bad choice, if you don't mind my saying so." The big head wobbled. "For a woman, I mean. Why not Family?"

Moxxanne had a confidence beyond her years and it showed. "I like action," she said, a big positive smile.

Roger's hands dropped limply to the table. "And you're doing what, some kind of literary thing on Harry for Ryerson Press?"

"Exactly."

He didn't seem convinced, "You've come a long way."

Moxxanne had a thing with men where she snuggled forward and practically inhabited the table, invariably making it intimate. "I'm only looking for background," she said innocently. "How Harry relates to Gaylord and how Gaylord relates to him. You see?"

He brushed his double chins. "I'm not sure I do, but I've known Harry since he bought his house and that must be thirty years ago." He spread his hands framing the moon face. "He's a fixture here in Gaylord, you know, the prodigal son returned and all that." The big head wobbled. "But you know what that's like, you get little appreciation in your own hometown. Is that the sort of thing you're looking for? Doesn't seem like much."

She had her elbows on the table, head resting on her hand, a fetching pose. "Oh, but it is what I want."

"I see," Roger said glancing at his watch. "How well do you know Harry?"

"Not at all. I've published stories on him previously but this time Ryerson wants more depth." She rubbed a thumb and forefinger together. "I expect to wrangle at least a credit out of it."

Roger was unimpressed, the big head wobbled. "Harry's a very private man, did you know that?"

"Of course. He's just out of hospital so I haven't been able to see him."

Roger scoffed, "He won't see you. Give your head a shake."

Moxxanne's green eyes twinkled merrily. "Oh, I think he will see me. What else can you tell me about him? And the town?"

Roger snuffled and mumbled, head wobbling. "See here, young lady, I really can't help you much on this. Harry is just another Gaylord citizen – I doubt many even know that he is an author." Then his piggy eyes went up, a new thought coming, "Did you know that most folks around here call him Joe Hollywood?"

Moxxanne nodded. "Yes, I've heard that."

"Well," he said, opening his hands, "that should tell you something. Harry was in Hollywood thirty years ago and after he came back the locals started calling him Joe Hollywood and it stuck. On the street, that's how they know him. Oh, and they also figured that he came back rich."

"And he did?"

"Eh? Oh I see. Well, if he didn't, he certainly returned better off than most, but this is Gaylord after all."

Moxxanne kept up her forward lean and engaging smile. "Gaylord folks don't particularly cotton to Harry?"

Roger's small mouth pursed. "Oh, we're not all that bad. I mean it works both ways. Harry's a loner. Drives around in that big black Lincoln and is not exactly an outgoing friendly person. He's private, lives in his big house and keeps to himself. So folks respect that. They leave him alone. He's earned himself that kind of consideration."

Moxxanne nodded and then frowned. "What about the fact that he's very ill right now? I'm told he might not make it."

Roger scoffed, "Harry has friends that care. Of course, he's is the type that is always missed after they're gone." His head wobbled. "Somehow that man has managed to fly under the radar all these years and not just here in Gaylord. I know who he is and so do many others, media folks and so forth." He spread his hands. "Harry's quite the thing, small town boy makes good. He's written a lot, his Zenith stuff is impressive, and you know, it's going to be a lot bigger."

"Really?"

The little mouth pinched. "Yes, I can't say more – confidential." He looked at his Rolex, "Hmm … I really must be—"

"Just one more quick one. Was Harry to blame for landing a plane in front of the hospital?"

The big fellow rocked. "Oh, that business. Well, that's all DOT stuff. Nothing to do with me – wouldn't tell you anyway."

Moxxanne pressed on "The press says DOT faults the pilot."

The huge body inched forward. The hands went out. "Nobody was hurt, the plane wasn't damaged and besides, Harry's an old man and he's got bigger problems than that right now." He put his hands on the table, "Is that about it, young lady?"

"Might you be referring to Harry's financial situation? Folks around here tell me he's busted."

The big face seemed to grow larger and a trifle unfriendly. "What do they know? Harry might even have a surprise or two left. You don't count that kind of man out, not even on his death bed."

The big fellow, with effort, pushed from the table. They shook hands and he waddled out.

Moxxane still had some latte. She reached into her satchel-purse and took out a tiny recording device. She switched it on and put it to her lips. Deftly she entered all the salient points of their conversation and then added a few notes of her own. She switched off and tucked it away, then she pulled out her smartphone from her biker jacket, in moments she was texting.

Yo! Kidney Bean! Wuzzup! Gettin' any?

Moxxanne drained her latte while she waited, and then, not so amazingly, the answering text appeared.

Hoo! Kidney Bone! What's it to ya?
Your neck will be broken!
Hah! Ya think? I'm lookin' for nookie!
Fugetaboutit!
No way! What's up in Gaylord?
Gaylord's a gas! Going for the works on Uncle Harry!
I'll bet! Don't crash and burn!

Moxxanne went out onto main street Gaylord and lit up a cigarette. It was freezing cold and quite snowy but it didn't seem to bother her. After a while she butted out and drove off in her rented Ford Mustang.

Chapter 18

"I'm glad you were able to accept my invitation, Moxxanne," Harry said. "Especially after I found you weren't really planning to interview me." Harry was seated behind his Yamaha electric piano.

"That's right, Uncle Harry," Moxxanne said. She was standing ten steps from the piano, large satchel purse dangling in front of her with both hands on the strap so that it almost touched the India rug. She wore her biker jacket but looked stunningly different this afternoon because she was sans the dazzling, silver blonde hair, which Harry had never seen but had heard about through Orson.

"Drop your stuff on the chesterfield and come over here," Harry said. His voice was scratchy but not unfriendly.

Moxxanne shucked her jacket and bag and stepped to the piano, putting one hand on the top board and looked around. " You got some library."

Harry shrugged and ran a thumb down the keys, the turned up volume making the notes reverberate in the high ceilinged room. "Forty years of collecting for fabricating eighteen works of fiction, so this is a working library." Harry had on a maroon dressing gown over pajamas, even though it was three in the afternoon, his bare feet encased in plain, black slippers. His dingy grey hair was as uncombed as usual and hung lankly over his forehead.

"You're not wearing your blonde hair," he commented without looking up.

Indeed she wasn't. Moxxanne put a hand up to her wavy red hair, a true carrot top, and for those her knew her both ways, the change was startling. "I left my disguise back at the motel," Moxxanne said. "I'm not here playing my investigator reporter role. It's just me, accepting your invitation."

Harry looked up and the piano went silent. "Orson called you a bombshell. An old-fashioned term, but then, Orson is old fashioned."

"So what do you think, Uncle Harry? Am I a bombshell?" She stepped back with her hands on her hips. She was wearing a green V-neck sweater with long sleeves pulled up almost to the elbows, a tall girl, red hair wavy to the nape, wide eyes more green than blue, and showing both confidence and mischief. She wore a black skirt, taut over the full hips and a trifle too short. The long legs were shapely and bare as were her lustrously-green toenailed feet, the snow boots having been left in the hall.

Harry plonked notes. "I don't call young ladies bombshells," he said looking her up and down. "I would call you beautiful."

"Naw," she protested. "People don't call me that, it's usually the other thing, you know, like, hey babe, and that's not so flattering."

Harry began leafing through sheet music. "Let's see. Since we haven't met before, I'm going to play you one of my songs. I'm told you're a bright law student so this should let you know a little bit more about me. Agreed?"

Moxxanne smiled, mouth wide in her long but decidedly pretty face.

"I'd love it," she said.

"I mostly write unrequited love songs," Harry said as he searched, "but let's not do that for you. Ah, here's one. I call it, "The Big Ole Moon." My voice is shot but you'll get the idea."

Harry lessened the volume on the Yamaha and then began to play and sing softly, the tune having a slight reminiscence of Neil Young.

Under that big ole moon,
Our love will come shining through,
I'll be there for you,
As long as the stars will shine,

Why don't you come walk with me,
We'll make love our destiny,
Side by side – each step of the way,
Our love will come shining through,

Under that big ole moon,
Our love will come shining through,
I'll be there for you,
As long as the stars will shine.

Harry ended the song by repeating the last verse and then stopped abruptly, snapping shut the piano top.

"Wow, Harry! That was great! It reminded me of Neil Young."

Harry got up and reached for his cane. "You caught that. It is a tribute. Let's go to the table."

The reading table dominated the centre of the carpeted library and had six high-backed leather chairs. Moxxanne and Harry sat in the middle, opposite each other. Gentleman Jack, branch water, glasses and cigars sat on a tray. Harry managed one of his slim smiles. "Orson tells me you're a drinking lady," he said with the hint of challenge. "But I can get you something else if you like."

Moxxanne settled in. She had jade bangles on her right arm. She eyed the amber booze. "I'll take a couple of fingers and a splash of water."

Harry's hand was fairly steady this afternoon, he poured then added water. He picked up a cigar. "Orson said tobacco doesn't bother you?"

Moxxanne brushed back the red hair. "Orson tells you a lot, doesn't he."

"Forty years of friendship. Want a Christo? They're mild."

She held out two fingers, into which Harry placed a cigar. There was a big ashtray between them.

They were both smoking and drinking.

"You didn't come to Gaylord to interview me. I was never part of it. Right, Moxxanne?"

"I did want to talk to you, Uncle Harry, but then, I found you were ill and weren't seeing anybody."

Harry gazed through cigar smoke. "Research is too easy these days. I checked Ryerson's archives on an essay you did two years ago. Did you have your blonde wig when you went to Cornish, New Hampshire?"

Moxxanne laughed and wiped her mouth with a table napkin. "That was before I joined Pegasus Theatre so I didn't have it yet. The wig business is just for fun. Like when you're a kid. You know, trying to fool people? My mother said I was a devil but after all, people have been wearing wigs for centuries. The blonde hair lets me feel so theatre and I'm the main character. What could be more fun? Orson didn't catch on so I finally told him. But Alva got it, didn't take her long."

Harry nodded. "Alva may be the smartest person in Gaylord." He paused several seconds, staring at her. "So that Cornish business. You didn't get to meet Salinger either."

She blew smoke. "Why meet Salinger? I'm not a Catcher in the Rye nut. I was after the Cornish thing. Salinger was like this elephant in the room but everybody somehow pretended he wasn't there. It was about that weirdness – that sort of contrived alienation. You could say that I'm into alienation because it's so difficult to write about. My essay was published – but it was kind of a hit and miss."

Harry rolled his cigar between thumb and forefinger. "You didn't miss by much. Ryerson covered your expenses?"

"Sure, but I had to sell the idea. I'm good at that – selling ideas."

"I'll bet you are. How did you sell them on coming to Gaylord? I'm hardly Salinger."

They were on refills.

"Maybe not but it's sort of the same – Gaylord pays little or no attention; you're part of the scenery. Mind you, the rest of the country treats you about the same."

She tapped the ash off her cigar. "Ryerson Press will publish but it's an English department project. Oh yeah, I also hope to pick up another writing credit towards my law degree."

Harry pressed knuckles to his eyes and then looked up. "None of my books have been big," he said, "and the movies, B's." He pointed the cigar. "This is quite a comedown from Salinger."

Moxxanne made her cigar glow and then waved the smoke away. "You're way too modest, Uncle Harry. How many Canadian writers can match what you've accomplished? The Zenith movies have gone big offshore. But you're right, I didn't come here for that. I didn't get it right at Cornish, that alienation thing, but I've got a good shot at nailing it here in Gaylord. I feel like I've got you and the town under a microscope. I just need a couple of more days."

She levelled the cigar. "So now you tell me something, Uncle Harry. Why did you want to see me?"

Harry touched his forehead. "Orson said I was missing out. He said you were a walking energy stick. Besides, it turns out we're related. True?"

Moxxanne tapped the stogy on the lip of the ashtray, amusement playing across her face. "You're going on Orson's say so?"

Harry shook his head. "You said, Early, but you didn't tell him which Early."

"My father's name is Early."

"That's right, but so is your grandfather's. Early Jr. must be your father – donated sperm or not."

"Orson couldn't figure that out?"

"Orson doesn't sweat the details but I do, so I spoke to my brother Early – your grandfather. It was an awkward question. You see, I'm not close to my brother. Anyway, he refused to confirm or deny.

Moxxanne shrugged. "I'm not close to my rich grandfather either"

"People around here think I'm the one with the money but the folks in Dauphin know better. Early is the rich brother."

"So are you saying that you didn't know about me before this?"

Harry rubbed his forehead again and then looked up. "My nephew has always been a hard guy to keep up with and your grandfather is private, especially where I'm concerned, so maybe I got left out of the loop. I'm sorry, Moxxanne. This is a helluva way for a family to operate." This time the smile was gone.

"I missed out on having a father and folks on your side of the family don't know me."

Harry stared for a moment. "So it's about you. You're the alienated one."

Moxxanne's smile came back and she shrugged. "Don't take me for some kind of crushed youth. Yeah, I was brought up by a single mom, big deal, it just made me a little more curious about what makes folks tick. That's why I went to Cornish. I had an itch, and that's why I'm here in Gaylord."

Chapter 19

Dr. Brian Schiller told Harry to roll his wheelchair closer to his desk. The clinic was on the main floor and Orson had been able to wheel him straight in, so now Harry and the doctor were alone together like they had been so many times in the past. The doctor pulled his half glasses further down his nose and peered over them, his brown eyes had gone slightly rheumy in what was now his seventy-fourth year, only one less than Harry, but he still had all his hair although now dull white and flat against his skull. He was a small man, ferret like, sinewy and with more pep than most folks his age. There was a glowing computer screen in front of him but his right hand lay flat on a sheaf of papers. He now tapped them with a forefinger.

"We're slowly learning to figure out what your body is up too, Harry, because it's clever at hiding its secrets." He took the glasses off and laid them on top of the papers, and then rubbed his balled fists into his dark eyes. He leaned back, looking up at the ceiling. "I just had a long conversation with Winnipeg St. Boniface Hospital."

His gaze dropped, engaging Harry eye to eye. "As you know, your tests all went to the Mayo Clinic for analysis and now the results are in, and it confirms what we suspected."

He paused, nodding affirmatively.

Harry was wearing a curling sweater against the December chill and his slender forearms were resting against the arms of the wheel-chair, it seemed an effort for him to hold his head up, and he looked goggle-eyed through his glasses. Long illness had shrivelled him but he still managed a glum smile. "How long have I got, Doc?"

Dr. Schiller held up a hand. "Don't get ahead of me, Harry, I need you to pay attention to this because it is precarious and I'll need you to make some decisions but not necessarily right now." He paused, mouth clenched, the question in his eyes.

"Fine by me," Harry said, still the combined frown and smile.

"Mayo confirms that you have a damaged heart and it's worsening, getting critical."

He picked up the top page and scanned it, like he was reconfirming, just to make sure. "We didn't get it initially because it was well hidden, an old injury at the back of your heart, it only shows up as a small dark area but Mayo confirms its true significance. It acts like a dead spot, a dead spot that is supressing your heart's ability to function properly." He put the nose glasses back on. "Untreated, you probably don't have long at all. Your heart will suddenly freeze on you."

Harry nodded, "No wonder I've been dreaming about pearly gates lately." He touched an unsteady hand to his pallid face. "An old injury you say? I wonder how that could be?"

Dr. Schiller shrugged. "It could have happened anytime, Harry. Those car wrecks of yours. Sports injuries. Something so violent that it probably made you lose consciousness. Can you remember?"

Harry frowned, his face pinching. "Lemme see … I've been brought in unconscious just one time. You were my doctor then, too. Jeez, it's a long time ago, probably twenty-five years."

"Really? How so?"

"I was playing old timer's hockey at the Gaylord Civic Centre and I ran into one of my own defenceman. When I woke up, I was in the Gaylord Hospital and you were standing over me."

Dr. Schiller was pondering, going back in time. "That long ago … the file for that would have been boxed up years ago. But I do believe I remember, yes, it just so happened that I was at the hospital for another patient and they brought you in unconscious."

He touched his right hand to his chin. "I began formulating an emergency procedure." He paused, the memory flooding back. "Possibly venting your head and all that stuff, no fun at all, especially back then in Gaylord – would have had to pack you in ice and send you to Winnipeg."

He shook his head at the remembrance. "I was just about to start emergency instructions, and you opened your eyes just like that. You said, 'Where the hell am I?' or something to that effect. Amazing. We kept you overnight for observation and then let you go – no reason not to."

"I never felt any different after that, Doc, not a bit. You think that could've been it?"

"Possible. That must have been some hit to do that. A thing like that could have made a scar corrugation at the back of your heart, not big enough to be detected, especially back then, but that damage seems to have come back to haunt you, Harry."

"So I've had it?"

Dr. Schiller leaned back and put his hands behind his stethoscoped neck. "No, no, we can't say that. This kind of thing is rare, very rare, hardly ever detected, but Mayo does have a procedure. They tell me it's almost the same thing as vulcanizing a tire, they put a patch over the corrugation, treat it as if it were a hole, but it is still a highly risky business, Harry, no guarantees for sure."

Harry frowned, pain in his face.

"Yeah, but if you're throwing me a lifebuoy, Doc, I'll sure as hell grab it. Whaddya figure my chances would be?"

Now Dr. Schiller frowned, "I'm not advising you to take it; it's probably less than fifty-fifty, especially at your age and condition. No, Harry, as your doctor I cannot recommend it. Your chances of living longer are better the way you are right now."

Harry didn't hesitate. "Thanks, Doc, that's probably good advice. Can you actually send me to Mayo?"

"No. Here's the thing. It turns out that one of their top guys does this kind surgery out of the Vancouver General. He's back there now – you'd be one of his trial cases – a sort of a guinea pig. Bear in mind what I said about the risk."

"Can you send me to Vancouver?"

Dr. Schiller took off his glasses and plopped them on the desk and then held his hands up. "Even after what I told you?" He shook his head. "Don't do it, Harry." More slow head shaking.

Harry was wearing his sour smile but sparks showed in his beady eyes. "Doc, I'll take what I can get. If this vulcanization thing works, did they tell you what I can expect to get out of it?"

"If it works – and that's a big if – you could expect a long recovery period, open heart surgery is no joke, but then you should be stronger with a heart that has some integrity." He sighed and shook his head. "Once again, Harry, I can't advise it."

"Thanks, Doc. I appreciate that." He leaned back in his wheelchair, gripping the arms. "How soon can you send me to Vancouver?"

Dr. Schiller saw Harry's resolve. He shrugged and steepled his fingers. "Okay, Harry, like they say, it's your funeral. I will do what I can to expedite this for you."

Chapter 20

Harry fell gasping out of his bed, clutching his throat, suddenly awake and fighting for his life, panic rising up and exploding in his brain and he thought he was a goner — this was it.

He awoke half an hour later, flat on his bedroom floor but seemingly breathing normally, everything good again, no racing heartbeat and thunder in his ears, only the outside rattle of tree branches against the side of his house; an early morning north wind had set to work, maybe that's what woke him. He was surprised at his weakness but managed to claw his way to a sitting position on his king sized bed, where he sat in the dark gathering back some strength, and his mind came back to it, the recurring nightmare, always the same, the Nitehawk falling out of the sky over Gaylord. He shuddered and tasted fear bile in his throat. He fumbled in the darkness and got his bedside lamp on. The nightmare had been running at its usual time, between two and three a.m., and now there was nothing to do but flee the bedroom and get over to his writing room just across the hall.

Harry pulled his robe closer over his ever more spindly frame and looked out the upstairs den window onto Ferguson Street; there was a streetlight there and he watched snowflakes angle down out the darkness and touch his window. The next things were done without even thinking about it, carefully pushing his slippered feet under the big oaken desk and taking his place on his comfortable swivel chair where he had sat for more than thirty years. The bottle of Gentleman Jack was there, three-quarters full and so was a glass.

He poured. There was also his humidor of Cristo Panatelas. He lit up. Both these actions were forbidden by his doctor. His thoughts went back and back. He was thirty-five years old again and working in the Gaylord Steel Rolling Mills. Incredible, forty years ago and it seemed like yesterday. Except for a handful of innocuous short stories that he'd managed to publish, his writing ambitions went unfulfilled, and he'd pretty much accepted his fate, that of just another Gaylord steel factory working stiff. It was New Year's, 1973, Friday, and he was at the pub getting drunk with Orson, his steelworker buddy, and that's when his life began to change.

Orson was thirty years old and had just started back at the steel mills after his pro boxing career had petered out. He had gone to Toronto to seek his fortune through boxing but there was no pot of gold at the end of that rainbow, and now, after eight years, he was back where he had started, the Rolling Mills. They'd told each other their life stories, the failed aspirations, and now the life of booze and drudgery. They spend hours talking about Orson's pro boxing matches as a welterweight fighter and how he had just needed one or two breaks that never came, and now he was married and his chance for escape was gone. Orson had the face of a boxer, the pug nose and spidery lines through his eyebrows, but he didn't talk like a fighter, he didn't talk like a fighter at all. In fact, it was Orson who was the social man of words, not Harry, who could be reticent in company. And Orson was well read, probably more so than Harry, and so in the bar it was like they were reversed, Orson wordy and well-spoken while Harry was the quiet one. Of course Orson knew of Harry's writing aspirations, his minimal successes, which now seemed to have reached a dead end. Another rainbow with no pot of gold.

But Orson had gotten an idea. He was a reader and had come upon an article at the Gaylord library: a printing company out of Collingwood, Ontario, was running a fiction contest, and Orson had pulled the notice off the bulletin board and took it home with him. Little did he know it was about to change their lives.

At first Harry had wanted nothing to do with it – entering contests was not his thing – but Orson persisted, wouldn't let it go. The Patterson Printing Co. had a publishing arm, Collingwood Publishing, and it was definitely the smaller part of the Patterson printing business. They had a small stable of Canadian fiction writers and were looking to develop a few more – hence the fiction writing contest, which was to be original work not to exceed fifty thousand words or two hundred pages. First prize would be a published book and perhaps the opportunity of more – other prizes were neither here nor there. Orson knew that Harry had a more or less completed novel – it had been in their pub conversations a number of times – and now he pressed Harry to finish it and enter it in the contest.

Harry's book had the working title, The Relentless Gun, and he himself considered it a corny novel. It was set in and around Gaylord back in the 1870s at the time of the Red River Rebellion and the emergence of Louis Riel, but there was little factual history in the novel. Harry's hero was a kind of a Casablanca Rick who owned a sawdust-on-the-floor bar in the Red River Colony, and had to walk the line between the Brits and the Métis. Of course, he had to be iron fisted and quick with a gun, Red River being as frontier as you can get. And of course Red River Rick had to go and make things doubly dangerous by getting involved with one of the daughters of a high official in the Hudson's Bay Co. Rick, being a Métis, this situation could not be allowed to stand. Big trouble ensued and unfortunately several HBC lads lost their lives in front of Rick's relentless gun, hence, the title. This was definitely not allowed to stand and Rick was forced to flee into the wilderness taking the fetching daughter with him. All did not end well.

Orson took it upon himself to get the manuscript packaged up and took it to the post office, and for some time nothing more was heard, and Orson thought that would be the end of it, and it nearly was because it did not win first prize or in fact any prize at all. Orson and Harry made little further mention of this supposed lost cause – until six months later when Collingwood Publishers sent a letter saying that they would prefer not to return the manuscript but instead wanted Harry to go to Collingwood for an interview.

Orson insisted that he should go along and act as Harry's agent – that's the kind of guy that Orson was.

It was the beginning of the beginning, and how fast five years flew by, five years that saw Harry publish a total of three novels, all in the western genre. The first one, The Relentless Gun, the one that Harry thought to be crap, was picked up by a shrimp-sized Hollywood Indie company called Advent Film Works. Thus far, Harry had made peanuts out of his published novels and still held down a regular shift at the steel mills as did Orson.

There was another meeting in Collingwood and again Orson went along as agent, which went well because they negotiated a pretty fair deal for Harry – one that would eventually lead to Harry becoming a kind of king fish in the fairly small pond of Gaylord. Advent did make a movie roughly based on Harry's book and renamed it, Red Blood, and it did little or no box office in North America but did surprisingly well abroad, which was what Advent Film Works was aiming for.

Harry did get some money this time and Orson got a little too, but the boys still worked at the mill. The real payoff came three years later, 1981, when Harry was forty-three years old. There was another trip to Collingwood and the Patterson Printing Co. And this time they put together a deal that was to secure Harry's foresee-able future. Orson did okay but had to keep on working at the mill. Advent Film Works and Collingwood Publishing were going into the sci-fi business – a series of books would be needed – and it turned out that Harry was just the man to do it. It was to be called the Zenith project. Harry would eventually become something of a millionaire – and Orson would keep on working at the mill.

Chapter 21

The door was open to Harry's upstairs den, just like Orson said it would be, and Moxxanne walked right in, and there she was, face to face with Harry, who was at his desk, hunched over, elbows on the oaken top. He was gimlet eyed but not scowling, not smiling either. An open bottle of Gentleman Jack was by his right hand and two empty glasses by his left. He made no greeting, only taking the Cristo cigar from his thin lips and waving her to the soft chair in front of the desk. The blinds were half drawn so only partial slanting afternoon sunlight was entering the otherwise bleak room. It was twenty below outside and the sunlight didn't seem warming. Harry was wearing a purple housecoat and had a white towel around his neck.

Moxxanne shrugged out of her black biker jacket and dropped it on the floor. She was barefoot, winter boots stowed at the front door. There was no carpet in Harry's room, just cold hardwood but it didn't seem to bother her. She was wearing a red V-neck with the sleeves pulled up to the elbows, no makeup and no jewellery. Her tight fitting jeans had seen better days but on her every day was a good one.

Moxxanne crossed her legs and sat back. The chair was oak, matching the desk, but with a comfortable cushion and solid side arms. She brushed her silver blonde fake tresses back from her shoulders while giving Harry her cross between a smile and a smirk – there no was deference being made here to the supposedly respected writer. There was nothing tidy about Moxxanne, her five foot nine inches looked all of that even when she was sitting down.

With a shaky right hand Harry poured a shot into each glass and then ever so carefully eased one across the desk, then he pointed to the carafe of ice water. They both helped themselves.

Harry drank and then spoke. "You're late. It's about time you showed up."

Moxxanne tugged her heavy chair closer to the desk and put her glass down, then her elbows, so that they were now practically eyeball to eyeball. "How do you know I showed up for you, Uncle Harry?" Moxxanne said, her lips tugged down in a pretty smirk.

Harry put his liver spotted hands on the desk, appreciation in his rheumy eyes. "Orson told me about your alternative theatre work and your fondness for using props and going around incognito and so forth." Harry's voice was not far off being normal, except for some scratchiness and noticeable lack of power.

Moxxanne put her long fingers into the wig, fluffing at it, the beginnings of a real smile starting to show. "For me it's not a prop – it's more like a woman's fancy, you know, like a fabulous hat." Her smile brightened. "If it bothers you, Uncle Harry, I'll take it off."

Harry's thin lips bent, bony shoulders hunched. "I see what you mean – a favourite hat." He waved a hand, "You're welcome to take it off, if you want."

Gracefully Moxxanne freed the wig and dropped it onto her biker jacket, then she put her fingers into her own thick red hair and began fluffing it out. It wasn't quite so full as the wig or even as long, but it was surprisingly the same, only unabashedly red.

"How do you like it?" she said, a real smile this time.

Harry rubbed a hand thoughtfully along his sagging jaw line, then nodded, "Lovely," he said, and then repeated, "Lovely."

They sat nursing their drinks, only a little over three feet of oak between them, like they were making a mutual inventory of each other.

"I don't see the resemblance," Harry said. "My nephew, Early Jr. – your father – he has dark hair."

"He's only my father biologically – at least that's what my mother tells me. Being a real father to me was never part of the deal," Moxxanne said flatly.

Harry nodded, a slim smile. "But you met him, did you not?"

"Sure I did – when I was just a little kid. He was my mother's pal from Ryerson and he visited a few times. My mother never told me about their, ah, arrangement until I was eleven."

Harry nodded and butted out the Cristo. It seemed to pain him to smile but he did. "I know your mother from Patterson Press."

"Of course." The wry smile "Just friends?"

Harry held her gaze. "And you worked for Patterson Press."

"I did. I read your books on my coffee breaks." Moxxanne went back to the full smirk. "My mother was your editor on the two Zenith books."

"That's how we met. Your mother is Gertrude Bachalder's strongest editor."

Moxxanne picked up a bronze paper weight from the desk top and began to toy with it. It was the four-inch Ferrari figure of a prancing horse. "How well do you know my mother?" she said coyly.

Harry clasped his hands. "There's a lot of your mother in the Zenith books – both our sweat and tears."

Moxxanne had her tongue in her cheek and nodded knowingly – there was a look in her eyes.

Harry didn't bite.

Chapter 22

A glum looking guy was staring out the parking lot window of his auto shop business. It was awhile before lunch and he had everything under control and so now was able to just sit behind his desk and wait for the next job to show up, sometimes on the hook of a tow truck and sometimes by the customers themselves. His medium-sized auto shop was located in an industrial park just west of Gaylord. His hunger pangs were growing and now he looked at his wall clock – 11:30 a.m., then he saw a newer Ford Mustang enter the parking lot, turn left and come to a stop in front of his window.

The girl that got out was tall, wore a black biker jacket, had on newfangled curvy sunglasses and had glamorous blonde hair – good looking young dame to be sure, the kind that automotive boys had fantasy dreams about and that were flaunted on wall calendars. He watched her take her purse, a large one, out of the car and dangle it off a shoulder.

The inside office door was open and now Gus Boychuk craned his neck for the girl to enter. She came right in and put her bag on the desk.

"Hi," she said, "My name's Moxxanne."

She had one of those longer facial shapes but this too emphasized the brightness of her smile. Her right hand went out smoothly and Gus obliged. She plopped herself down on the only chair in front of the desk.

Gus tugged on his hat, one that had the logo of the Winnipeg Jets hockey team, and he stayed glum. He wore coveralls up to his neck and naturally, being an auto shop, they were indifferently clean.

Moxxanne unzipped the bike jacket and leaned so that her bosom touched down on the desk. "You gotta be the boss – your name is?" She had amped up the smile even more.

Gus had no chance against this type of dame, he was a smart but sad sack guy. "Gus," he said. His name was actually Gustave after his maternal grandfather who had first started the business many years ago.

"Oh, that's one of my favourite names." Then she held up a cautionary palm. "I'm only staying for a couple of minutes of your time, Gus, is that okay?"

Gus nodded glumly – no doubt she was a sales person and probably new on the job, besides, women were rare in automotive. He waited for her to dive into her large purse.

"I'm from Ryerson University, Toronto."

Gus nodded, baffled.

"I'm here on behalf of our newspaper – Ryerson Press? We're doing a series of articles, almost a bio, on one of your fair city's favourite sons – a man I'm told you've helped a lot through your business over many years. He's the writer, Harry Breen?"

So that's it, Gus thought. It would have to be Harry who brings a reporter to my door – better get rid of her quick.

Moxxanne nudged her tits forward. "You're a friend of Harry's – right, Gus?"

Gus had a waxy complexion that enhanced his naturally glum look. He tugged his cap. "Umm ... sure, but I got lots of customers."

Moxxanne made a thing out of brushing blonde strands off her face and then adjusted the sunglasses perched on top. "Ryerson Press is a big fan of Harry's and he has a ton of fans in our readership. We're looking for interesting background, you know, like his important hobbies? You look after his automobiles, don't you, Gus?"

Maybe it wasn't going to be that bad Gus was thinking, answer a few questions and get rid of her. "Umm ... yeah ... I'm not sure what you want to know."

Moxxanne pushed back and crossed her legs. "We already know a lot about Harry, for instance his motorcycles – what kind of motorcycle?"

Gus knew plenty, he'd been looking after Harry's bikes for more than twenty-five years. "Umm ... only one kind – Honda Goldwing."

"Why a Goldwing?"

"Huh? Oh I see – it's a big touring rig. Harry rode them all over the place. He rode around Gaylord a lot too."

"So would he be, like, a biker?"

"Naw, Goldwing guys are motorcyclists."

"And the cars?"

"Nissan 300Z's. He drove those all over, too." Gus frowned. "But he hasn't been around lately. Not since he landed that airplane in front of the hospital."

"Oh yeah, I want to ask you about that. But first, what kind of rider and car driver was Harry? I've heard some stories around town."

"Oh? Like what?"

"Accidents and stuff. Could you tell me about that?"

Gus tugged at his cap like he did when he was stalling. "Harry had his favourite roads around Gaylord. Lotta gravel. Those Nissan 300's are sports cars – you need those kind of roads – not so much the Goldwings – but Harry drove them on gravel too."

"Sounds dangerous."

"Oh yeah. We brought Harry back on the hook a number of times."

"The hook?"

"Yeah, tow truck."

"Was he hurt?"

"Only when he rolled a Nissan. A Goldwing went down too. Gravel can be bad for big bikes. But Harry had good riding gear

– so he mostly got roughed up. That's what these guys do – slide around on gravel on the banked corners. That's where they get into trouble – slide off the road."

"You say guys? You mean there's like a club or something?"

"Naw, not a club, just guys around Gaylord who drive like that, but Harry's a loner – likes to do his own thing."

"I see, but nothing since that aircraft thing I keep hearing about."

"That's right, nothing since Harry landed in front of the Gaylord hospital."

Chapter 23

Moxxanne got out of her rented Ford Mustang at Sheffield Airport which was seven miles south of Gaylord and was surprised at how big it was, lots of commercial hangars and smaller planes, and even what seemed a substantial helicopter operation, but she had found the right hangar, which had a big overhead sign that read, Holms' Building Co., but she could tell at once that it was all about small aircraft. The wide hangar door was open and she walked in and immediately met a guy carrying a clipboard.

"Could you tell me where I can find Leonard?"

"I'm Leonard. And you must be?"

"Moxxanne. Yeah, I phoned earlier."

He stared at her, like most men did, she with the big, silver blonde hair, tall and fullness of figure that showed even though she was wearing a biker jacket.

"Right. You wanted to talk about Harry."

"I did. I won't take up much of your time."

He looked at his watch. "I got a student to take up in twenty minutes – will that do?"

"Perfect."

The office was a bare bones affair that you'd expect on an airfield site, and Leonard was that too, a chubby man around sixty with a ruddy complexion and grey hair showing under his dark ball cap that had some kind of flying insignia on it. He gave up his clipboard laying it on his uncluttered desk.

He smiled and his light eyes were friendly. "Okay, shoot."

Moxxanne shucked her jacket and then pulled her chair up and snuggled closer to the desk, her green blouse was V-necked and showed generous cleavage, even more so when she put her elbows on the desk so that her boobs touched down and long graceful fingers folded under her pretty face.

"Thank you so much for having me. Like I told you earlier, I'm a law student from Ryerson but I'm also a lead reporter for our campus paper and we're doing a feature story on Harry so I just have a few questions for you."

Most men couldn't stop looking at Moxxanne's tits and now Leonard's ruddy face got even rosier. He reached for his clipboard like he might need protection. "I've known Harry for a long time," he managed, finding his mouth dry.

Moxxanne snuggled closer, she enjoyed the close proximity of working men. "It's about Harry and that Nitehawk incident that happened in Gaylord about two years ago?"

"Oh that. Do you mind if I smoke?"

"Nope."

He put the clipboard down and lit up and then as an after-thought, "Oh sorry, you want one?"

"Don't mind if I do." She reached out two fingers into which Leonard placed a cigarette. He held up a gold lighter that also sported an aviation insignia.

Leonard inhaled gratefully, coughed a bit and began. "Yeah, we had this situation with Harry and the Nitehawk. Harry landed it on the highway right in front of the Gaylord Hospital. That's what you want, eh?"

Moxxanne blew a stream of blue smoke, "That's the one, yes."

Leonard tugged at his buttoned collar, he wore an old-fashioned bow tie. "We never could figure what happened. Harry swore to me that the Nitehawk quit – both engines – which you gotta under-stand that's practically impossible on that particular aircraft. The black box in that thing wasn't conclusive, you see, Miss, ah …"

"Moxxanne."

"Moxxanne … the aircraft was running perfectly on that highway, wheels down and everything. It don't make sense, not with Harry flying. Oh, he took it hard, very hard, and I haven't seen him since." He scratched his clean shaven chin. "Ya know, I miss the guy, everybody does. He was kind of a fixture around here." He glanced at his watch.

"Harry was a good pilot?"

"On the Nitehawk? The best. Thing was, he loved that aircraft. I mean he really loved it. I know damn well he was jealous of it."

"Jealous of an airplane?"

"Oh yeah, see some guys are like that. Our operation is strictly co-op – owned by the membership, and our aircraft are pretty much all leased, like the Nitehawk was. I liked it but Harry loved it – but only a few of our seasoned members cared for it – too much new technical stuff and it wasn't all that user friendly. Harry and I went down to Denver around five years ago and picked it up. We got checked out on it and then flew it back to Gaylord, Harry in the right seat. But by the time we got home Harry was doing most of the flying and he landed it. The Nitehawk and Harry were love at first sight. He couldn't get enough of it – even hung around and helped out with the maintenance."

He took a last drag before butting out. "Coincidentally the lease was up right after Harry had that supposed flameout thing. The guys voted not to renew so the Nitehawk went home to Denver. I phoned Harry but he didn't even want to come in and say goodbye. Funny, eh?"

Moxxanne nodded, she butted out too. "What's your take, Leonard? Was that emergency landing Harry's fault?"

Leonard checked his watch and picked up the clipboard again. He slowly made a few negative nods. "I know that aircraft and I know Harry. There's nothing to prove it except Harry's word but here's what he maintains happened. You see, Harry volunteered to do easy check pilot work for Denver Aviation, the company that built the Nitehawk. He wasn't acting as a test pilot or anything like that, it was just routine stuff straight out of the Nitehawk's flying manual. One of the check tests was a simple shut down and restart of the Nitehawk's two small turboprop engines. Harry and I have both done that test on the Nitehawk. Switch 'em off, wait ten seconds and then follow the manual procedure to switch 'em back on. Couldn't be simpler. The thing's computer controlled most of that so that's what Harry did. He climbed to three thousand feet, trimmed the aircraft and shut the turboprops down, waited the ten seconds then went through restart."

Leonard shook his head. "Harry's story is that the Nitehawk refused to restart – and believe me, the Nitehawk does not make much of a glider, it'll start losing altitude in a hurry." Leonard shook his head again, jaw clenched.

"If that's what happened – and Harry said it did – believe me, he'd hafta get back down on the runway in a hurry … except Harry can't remember much of what happened after the engines wouldn't fire. I guess his mind was racing and he was kind of busy. Somehow he wasn't able to orient back to the field like he shoulda done. Mind you, it was dark, and it's not easy to dead stick a plane like the Nitehawk."

Leonard shook his head again. "I'm thinking Harry was lost up there – fighting for his life – and found himself falling into Gaylord. It must have been terrifying. He swears he can't remember putting the Nitehawk down on the highway right in front of Gaylord Municipal Hospital."

Leonard shook his head one last time. "I've seen it before – pilot fog – when the crisis is over they can't remember exactly what happened. Anyway, DOT suspended Harry's licence and that's the way it still stands. The funny thing is, when the cops got there, the Nitehawk's turboprops were running perfectly. Too bad for Harry, because then who's gonna believe him? Harry thinks that before touchdown the Nitehawk came back to life and that's how he was able to get the wheels down. Makes sense too."

He stood up, slightly shorter than Moxxanne's five foot nine. He paused, "Did that help you?"

Moxxanne was pulling on the biker jacket. "Thanks a lot, Leonard, I really appreciate it." She took out her cell and began punching in numbers then putting it to her ear while still looking at Leonard.

"Do you mind if we talk again? I might have another question or two."

Leonard was already heading out the door with his clipboard and spoke over his shoulder. "Anytime, Moxxanne."

Chapter 24

"So what did you bring me?" Alva said, watching the girl set the brown bag down on the low coffee table.

"Johnny Walker. Not the best, but hey, I'm a student, eh," Moxxanne said, taking a seat on the dark leather sofa.

"Not my fav," Alva said, pulling it out of the bag, "but it'll do. You want ice?"

"Just soda water is good for me."

Moxxanne had left her biker jacket and satchel purse hanging in the hall. She was wearing a white cable knit sweater with a low V-neck, she seldom wore anything that didn't show off her cleavage asset. She wore tight jeans and white socks. Her youthfully smooth, pale complexion showed no makeup, only a modest lipstick shade. There was no jewellery, not even a ring on the elegant long-fingered hands. Her silvery blonde hair was almost too good to be true.

Alva put down whiskey glasses, a small pitcher of ice water, then she snapped the tab on a can of soda water. She uncapped the Johnny Walker and poured for them both, a good three fingers.

"So you call yourself an investigator?" Alva said taking the seat on the La-Z-Boy that was on the fireplace side of the table.

Moxxanne's soft smile turned into a wide toothy grin. "I do," she said waving a dismissive hand, "but that's part of my role playing. I'm having a lot of fun with this."

"Are you now. That seems cheeky."

"Oh, I'm sorry – I didn't mean it like that. You see I'm with Pegasus Theatre. Maybe you've heard of us?"

"No. Can't say that I have."

"Well, it's from Toronto and we're different, you know, because we do a lot of androgynous stuff?"

Alva swished her drink. "You don't say," she said.

"Yeah, cross dressing and all that, sometimes it's a girl playing a boy playing a girl? The audience has to guess – it's a lot of fun."

"I get it," Alva said, brightening. "The Julie Andrews thing – the sexual mix-up – drove James Garner nuts."

"Exactly. Well, I'm caught up with it – the theatre I mean – I'm even wearing something from our costume department. Can you guess?"

Alva grinned, obviously amused and taken with the antics of this young person. She shook her head laughing. "Underwear?"

"Not underwear," Moxxanne scoffed. "How could you see that?" Her voice had teenage exuberance but adult strength.

"It's the hair!" She clapped a hand over it, green eyes shining happily.

Alva put her drink down. "So! I wondered about that. To me that hair seemed almost too much."

"It is," Moxxanne laughed, "but I love it. I feel like Sherlock Holmes with his deerstalker. So I'm really into being an investigative reporter and I'm here to have fun with it." With that she burst into laughter and Alva was caught up in it and started laughing too.

Alva brushed hair back from her face, it had once been lustrously dark but was now sown with silver strands. "You kids are something else," she said, still giggling. "So how far does this androgynous stuff go? Are we talking gay theatre?"

Moxxanne stopped laughing but her eyes still shone. "Not necessarily, but hey, for me sex is like one of those pirate treasure chests? You open the lid and it's packed with rubies and pearls and all that stuff." Her pretty face sobered, "Am I shocking you?"

Alva shook her head, completely nonplussed. She waved a dismissive hand. "Of course not." She drained her glass and then poured for the both of them. "I look at you and I see myself forty years ago when I was at the University of Winnipeg, taking pharmacy and doing theatre myself." She touched her cheek; she still had an attractive face.

"Oh sure, I was a looker back then, just like you, not so tall but I had the equipment, and boy, didn't I know how to use it." She pointed a finger conspiratorially. "I know what it's like to stop men in their tracks – that's fun, isn't it."

"I bet you still could. You're still a lovely looking lady."

Alva was wearing a plain sweatshirt with long arms and she tugged one sleeve up over a studded bracelet. "Oh, that's all over now," she said, dark eyes narrowing. "Enjoy yourself young lady because it will end for you too. Enjoy every bit of it."

"I plan to," Moxxanne agreed and then said, "but it's plain to see why both Orson and Harry would be attracted to you."

Alva brushed the still mostly black flank of hair from her face again. "So let's get on with it – just what is it you want to know from me?"

Moxxanne's face became serious. "Our literature department is underwriting this trip. A couple of professors have taken a keen interest in Harry and Gaylord."

Alva touched at the beginning of a double chin. " I still don't see why."

"I wrote an essay about Harry two years ago when I was only a cub reporter. I was looking for writing points toward my law degree so I took on the Harry assignment not realizing that two years later it would lead me into an even better assignment here in Gaylord. All I've got to do is find out why Harry is such an enigma, not just here in Gaylord but a mystery man everywhere. The profs want me to come up with some answers." This time Moxxanne reached out and recharged both their glasses. The Johnny Walker was dying fast.

Alva shook her head. "He's no mystery to me."

"Here's the thing, three of his books have been made into movies, well, B movies, but still, how many Canadian writers can claim that? And he has published fifteen other books, again, no bestsellers, but he still did it, and he gets little or no recognition, especially here in his hometown of Gaylord? Apparently he can walk around freely and folks pay little or no attention to him – it's like he's just part of the woodwork."

Alva shrugged. "Maybe you've just answered your own question."

"How long have you known Harry?"

Alva put her glass down. There was a mirror over the fireplace mantle and now she stared up at it. "That would be like telling you how old I am." She smiled and the tiny wrinkles in her face lined up. "Let's see, I was just thinking the other day, oh, thirty or more years I guess." Her chin firmed up and she nodded pensively. "Aw, mostly good friends ... yeah, mostly good friends for that long."

Moxxanne leaned forward, an innocent expression. "You knew Orson first?"

Alva swished her drink. "If you write this crap I'll have to kill you."

"I won't write what you don't want."

"Orson and I have always been close. You're a big girl, figure it out. Harry, not so much. But that's how I met Harry, through Orson."

Moxxanne tapped a finger to her lip. "Okay, you and Orson are solid even now?"

"I will strangle you if you print this stuff."

Moxxanne shook her head "This is strictly girl talk."

"Are you surprised that older folks still get it on?"

"Not at all. I just wonder how Harry fits in this picture."

They both stared for a moment, neither speaking.

Finally Alva spoke. "Harry had his moments, but mostly I was his muse. I had to listen to most of his goddamn story plots even before he started to write them. Sure, he was a good friend. Sure, I liked him, so I did it."

She started looking up at the mirror again. "Being a muse, well, it's sorta like sex but a helluva lot less fun."

Chapter 25

Gus "Snuffy" Boychuk was standing in the fenced compound behind his Gaylord Industrial Park garage and body shop. He was pointing out a 2006 Nissan 350Z sports car that had a crushed left fender. Gus, medium height and portly in his mechanic overalls, had a ruddy jowly face and his once white painter's hat had seen better days. He had a throaty, muffled voice that suited his middle-aged looks.

"See here," Gus was saying, pointing to the crumpled fender, "this one ain't busted up too bad. Harry walked away from this one without a scratch but he wasn't so lucky with the first two."

The tall young blonde standing beside Harry was chewing and snapping bubble gum. It was a cold December day in Gaylord, -22°C, but the girl's black biker's jacket was unzipped and her leather gloves were fingerless.

"What other two?" she asked.

" Harry's been running these Zed's for years. I sourced them for him and got them road ready. The first one, a 300z, that was about twenty years ago – a good low mileage car. Well, Harry rolled that one, a complete write-off. Put 'im in the hospital. See, there's a lot of gravel roads around Gaylord and Harry loves gravel, makes the back end slide out, nice but dangerous as hell. So I sourced Harry another newer and even better 300z. So guess what, after a couple of years he rolled that one too – another complete write-off. So he's back in the hospital again. And then I sourced him this 350z. Like you can see, it's pretty nice. This one lasted him until a couple of years ago, like 2012, and then he pranged it. Not the same gravel road but one just like it. And there she sits. He hasn't said a word about it so I don't know what the hell to do with it. And now, maybe you heard? They say he's dying."

The tall girl snapped her gum again. "Yeah, folks have been telling me that. It's sad. Can we step inside, Gus? I've got a couple more questions."

Gus's office was typical, on the grimy side and with a requisite girly calendar on the wall. He picked up a pencil and started tapping his desk blotter. He was a man with a perpetual hang dog look, sad droopy eyes that made you wonder when he last smiled or if he still could. "I'm not sure what else I could tell you," he said.

Moxxanne was sitting in the chair in front of the desk. She exuded a confidence that went along with her looks and men usually gave her the double take. "Could you tell me how long you've known Harry?" she asked.

Gus tapped his pencil, "Oh, let's see, forever. I'm from Gaylord too. God, I knew Harry when he was still driving clunkers. I knew him before they started calling him Joe Hollywood. This ain't that big a place so everybody knows about Harry."

"So tell me, Gus – I would trust your opinion – what kind of a guy is Harry?"

Moxxanne's voice had youthful edginess, but the rest of her – that was all grown up.

Gus stopped tapping. "Ah geez. I'd say pretty regular and down to earth, but of course he is a mover."

"A mover?"

Yeah. You know – loves cars, motorcycles and airplanes. Been like that since I've known him. Only I haven't seen him for going on two years so I guess he's stopped at last."

Moxxanne popped her gum. "He stopped coming here just like that?"

"Yep. It was right after that airplane business. You heard about that?"

Moxxanne nodded. "Yeah, but not that much."

Gus's pencil started up again. "Well, see, a couple of years ago Harry lands this plane in Gaylord right in front the hospital. It was a perfectly good plane, still running and everything. The cops said it should have been damn near impossible for Harry to do that. There's trees and telephone poles along there. They say Harry was just sitting there, kind of dumbstruck. And that was it. They took him to the hospital and then he went home. After that he has hardly come out of his house. Can you beat that?"

Moxxanne shook her head. "No, I can't." She leaned back. "You've been great, Gus. I'm definitely gonna use some of this. Is it okay if I quote you, I mean use your name?"

Alarm came into Gus's sombre eyes. "Geez, better not. Folks might not like what I said."

Moxxanne hunched forward. "This is not going to be a bad story, Gus. It's the other way, a feel good story about Harry and Gaylord. You've just told it like it is and that's exactly what I'm looking for about Harry."

"Yeah? Geez, I hope I'm not sorry about this."

Gus walked her back to her rented Mustang.

Moxxanne pointed to the big sign over the building.

"How come it says, Tim's Tires and Paint?"

Gus shrugged. "I bought it that way thirty years ago and didn't see any need to change it." He shrugged again.

"Everybody in Gaylord knows me."

Chapter 26

"So it's Little Brown Jug this time, eh?" Alva said, pulling the stubby bottle of scotch out of the brown bag.

Moxxanne tossed her black biker jacket and satchel purse onto the couch, then brushed her silver blonde hair back from her face. "Best I could find on my budget," she said with her usual big smile. She wore no makeup accept for a hint of pale lipstick. She didn't need much being a young woman full of health and energy. She was wearing a green sweater, which matched the eyes and of course it was low cut. She settled into the comfortable armchair, the low coffee table between them, Alva on the twin chair opposite.

"It'll do," Alva said, cracking the cap. The glasses, ice water and soda were already there.

"So where were we?"

"You were telling how Harry got started."

"Oh yeah." She poured the drinks. "Well, I guess you really could say Orson started Harry's career. Like I told you, those two became friends at the Rolling Mills, drinking buddies. Of course Orson knew about Harry's writing and lack of success, only a bunch of rejection slips."

"So Harry was still unpublished?"

Alva took a sip and brushed her still mostly black hair from her face. "That's right, no success at all. It's funny, isn't it, how things are sometimes opposite from what you'd think? Here's Orson, an ex-prizefighter, and Harry, a wannabe writer, and which one do you think is at the library reading all the time? You guessed it, it's

Orson – a better reader than Harry ever was. So it was Orson, while at the library, who discovered that there was this publisher, well actually more of a printing press company, from Collingwood, Ontario, called Patterson's, that was running a fiction contest for unpublished writers.

"By this time Harry had just about given up, but Orson knew he had this novel with the working title, The Relentless Gun. Orson hadn't read it, didn't care much for Westerns, but I had. It wasn't great but good enough. The story was set around 1870 at the time of the Red River Rebellion. Harry's hero was a half breed cowboy, a reckless fool if ever there was one but spot on with a six shooter and a repeating rifle. Clint Eastwood should have had this. The cowboy tries to be neutral between the British and the half breeds. In the end, they all turn against him and he flees south of the border taking the Hudson's Bay factor's daughter with him. It's not a bad read if you like that sort of thing."

She brushed the hair from her face again and took a sip before continuing. "Turns out this old shoot 'em up may be one of the better things Harry's done. Orson grabbed the rough manuscript and sent it off to Patterson's. Probably Harry knew about it but pretended not to be interested. Well, it eventually got published and so began the writing career of Harry. The book didn't cause much of a splash, made practically no money – but here's the thing, this indie movie company from Hollywood, Advent Film Works, grabbed up the movie rights. Go figure. And three years later they made a B or C movie out of it. It too sank like a stone."

"And this made Harry successful?"

Alva shook her head as she poured new drinks. "That was just a start. Patterson's liked Harry and they made a writer out of him. Like I told you, Patterson's is primarily a printing press outfit with an in-house publishing arm, mostly Canadian fiction. Their managing editor is a woman, Gertrude Bachalder. She's probably around eighty by now. She has directed Harry's writing efforts, well, novel by novel. But they seldom meet, only when it was necessary for Harry to be in Collingwood and she has never set foot in Gaylord. This Gertrude woman is wheelchair bound, a widow – and probably without her – there is no Harry."

Moxxanne nodded, a knowing smile.

"She was tailor-made for Harry's writing. Harry put out stuff on her say so, westerns at first, I think seven in all, and then mysteries, about eight I think, and after that, the Zenith series, a trilogy, but only two got published. Zenith was sci-fi, two of which Advent made into chintzy movies." Alva paused and frowned. "But you must already know a lot about Harry's books and movies?"

Moxxanne stirred her new drink with her finger. "I've read Harry – the Zenith stuff – but I haven't seen the movies. But I've heard that there is new interest in Zenith. Did Harry make money out of this?"

Alva shrugged hair out of her face. "I'm not his accountant but no doubt he made dough out of Zenith, like maybe a million bucks, not bad for a yokel from Gaylord. That's what bought him Harry's house, sport cars, motorcycles and such."

Chapter 27

Right away Moxxanne saw that this was different – way different. Alva was in a white terry cloth robe. They were in the living room again with its big tyndal stone fireplace, which was blazing away – it was minus twenty degrees outside. Alva was laid part way back on her La-Z-Boy. It was obvious she'd already been into the sauce and the wall clock showed only 2:00 p.m. She'd started early. She wore no makeup and her eyes seemed puffy. Some crying going on? She clutched her glass, the open scotch bottle on the coffee table. Had Alva just been in the bathtub? Was that it? Her fuzzy robe was carelessly slack, framing cleavage.

"How many times does this make?" Alva said, voice thicker than usual. "Four? Or is five? Goddammit, haven't you got enough on that fuckin' Harry? He's just a shit you know."

She paused to finish her drink and then stooped to build another. No ice. Little soda. She sniffed, pulled a Kleenex and dabbed her nose.

She waggled a finger at Moxxanne. "He used me you know. I had to listen to all that Zenith bullshit. All three fucking novels. And I did it. Was I dumb or what?" She waited but Moxxanne didn't respond. "Okay. I did my best. I told him where I thought he was getting into pure bullshit."

She drank again. "Okay, you wanted to know, Harry used me for a sounding board. Of course it all went off to his editor and he made his million bucks. So you see little miss lawyer?"

Moxxanne had shucked her biker jacket and it lay on the floor. She had on a loose red top. If Alva was expecting some kind of sympathy she was getting only the fisheye.

"Aw, I see you're really interested."

She put her glass to her mouth – no lipstick. "Well, Harry was interested – with his goddamned books." She pointed the finger. "Writers – they're so fuckin'vain. Sure, he was using me – anyway he could." She put her thumb to her chest. "He thought he was doing me a favour, the asshole."

She leaned back and pulled her robe together. "Well, bugger that. Orson is better anyway. He cares about people." She paused, dark eyes levelling. "So what's up with you today? Cat got your tongue? Wrong time of the month?"

Moxxanne was wearing her faded jeans, bare feet on the floor, toenails bright red. She made no response to Alva, just the fisheye.

"Yeah, well, fuck you too," Alva said. She jerked forward, eyes darkening. "All that talk about going both ways. You kids think you invented that?" She stood up and cinched her robe, then spread her arms out.

"Where do you think all this came from? Because I'm an idiot? Sixteen condos here, baby, and I sold every goddamned one of them." She bent forward, cleavage opening. "I sold my drug store business and then these condos."

She waggled a thumb. "That's right, kid, I got bread – got a lot of it – so maybe I'm not Harry's dummy after all. Because now I hear he's broke and I'm the one with the dough."

She plopped back down, landing with a slap. "Whaddya think of me now, kid?"

Moxxanne sipped her drink but kept up the dismissive fish eye.

Alva carefully placed her glass on the coffee table, she didn't reload. "So that's how it is, eh?" Her pointy finger came out again. "Don't you kid yourself; you can't show me anything."

She paused, a challenging stare. "Don't you dare underestimate me. I could take you easy." She sat back pulling her knees up, bare legs together, then sneered and waved a palm disdainfully. "Your generation – all talk – no show."

There was a staring match that lasted for about half a minute, then Moxxanne put her drink down. She stood up and pulled off her red top. The jeans went next – she was commando, and no shave job. She pulled off the silver blonde wig and fluffed her own red hair. It wasn't quite as luxurious but somehow just as good, and, besides, it matched.

Alva clutched her knees, low voice having booze and excitement. "Oh boy, a girlie show. Maybe I spoke too soon." The dark was gone from her eyes and replaced by shine.

Moxxanne, lithe as a tiger, grabbed the hefty coffee table so that nothing spilt and moved it sideways.

Alva giggled, excited, nervous. "Just what do you think you're doing?"

Moxxanne was quickly upon her but did not speak. Deliberate and sudden. She took Alva by the ankles.

They stared into each other's eyes – a dare going both ways.

Moxxanne yanked her off the La-Z-Boy. The carpet was plush and the tall fireplace had a dancing fire.

Alva made defensive fists – but didn't punch. Instead she made giggling growls.

Moxxanne took the terry cloth – a rude unwrapping.

Alva was sixty-three and fleshy but every bit a woman. Moxxanne held her down by the shoulders.

Alva made feeble attempts to push free then stopped.

"Bitch!" she said huskily. "Bitch!"

Chapter 28

They were at the Oasis Trailer Park in Orson's double wide. It was late – after midnight and between the two of them they had killed a twelve-pack of beer. Orson was on his La-Z-Boy with his fuzzy, red-wool stockinged feet propped on an ottoman where an electric heater was blowing directly on them. It was twenty-three below outside. Moxxanne was sprawled on a divan so that there was around eight feet separating them. The double wide's living room was surprisingly spacious. This had been Orson's home for the past twenty-two years, which marked the time his marriage had broken up and he had henceforth lived as a bachelor.

Orson had a way of raising a finger and stabbing the air when he was about to make a declaratory statement. "You came to Gaylord to find out stuff, Moxxanne, that's brave, you want to face it, your past, your future – whatever. I don't want Harry should die on you and then you gotta leave empty handed. I could tell you some stuff – but it ain't good stuff – it's bad stuff. You want that?"

Slowly Moxxanne pushed herself to a sitting position, she had invested time and effort into Orson and now it might be paying off. She tugged at the powder blue top she was wearing, a little too much cleavage was spilling. The faded blue jeans with the ripped knees matched things up. She was barefoot but the cool floor didn't bother her.

"I'm all ears," she said. "Let's hear this bad stuff."

"It'll shock you – it's that bad. You sure you can take it?"

"Chrissake, Orson, C'mon."

"You've already visited your Uncle Harry, what? A half a dozen times since you've been here?"

"Yeah. So?"

"You like him a lot, don't you?"

"He's okay."

"Well, it's time you knew the facts. I'll take you back to the first Zenith movie when Harry and I went to Hollywood. Oh no, he wouldn't go on his own. I told you he's no good that way. I had to be with him and help him find his way in the world. Harry was there to assist on the movie script – me – I was just hanging around. So guess what? There's this Mexican girl that had a small part in the movie. Yeah you guessed it, Harry goes nuts for her like he always does with a new woman in his life. They date, but it turns out she's already got a thing going on with the number two director. It's Hollywood and the kid is just trying to get somewhere. I try to explain this to Harry and I think everything is okay but the next thing I know I get a call from the cops – they got Harry. At first they told me he'd tried to strangle the kid but then it turns out she decides not to press charges – says it was just one of those things. So Harry's out. But Advent Studios don't want him around anymore so we both head back to Gaylord. So you see? I'm just trying to tell you – your dear old Uncle Harry might not be what you think."

"Geez, Orson. So it's a love spat – a bit of rough trade going on. What's the big deal on that?"

Orson wriggled his fuzzy red toes in the rays of the glowing heater, and the table lamp had picked up on it and was reflecting a rosy glow to his face and bald head. All he needed was horns for his happy devil's face to be complete.

"I'm just trying to show you the trend, Moxxy."

His pointy finger came out again. "Did Alva tell you about the trouble she had with Harry?"

Moxxanne laughed and did her own finger pointing. "Oh, did you mean the ménage à trois you guys had going?"

Orson waggled his head and smirked. "You're new in town, Moxxy, that's neither here nor there. I'll bet that she didn't tell you that he punched her lights out and she ended up with raccoon eyes. Went around with dark sunglasses for a couple of weeks. That almost ended my friendship with Harry. See? I told you, he's not good with women."

Moxxanne frowned. "No, she never told me anything like that."

Orson folded his muscular old arms across his chest, a smugness to his pursed lips.

"Like the song says, Moxxy, you ain't heard nothin' yet. I got more – sure you want it?"

Moxxanne placed an empty beer bottle on the floor to make an even half dozen and then laced her long fingers together. She wasn't smiling. "You haven't forgotten that I'm in Gaylord as a reporter, have you, Olson?"

Orson shook his head. "Nope, but you're not going to print what I want to tell you anyway."

"Don't bet on that, Orson."

The gnarly finger came out again. He shook it this time. He leaned forward so that his face was more in the light. "I'm going to tell you about the manuscript for the second Zenith. Harry and I brought it to Collingwood around twenty-three years ago. You're twenty-two, right?"

Moxxanne nodded.

"Your mother, Della Lolly, edited the manuscript, with Harry of course. That work took maybe two weeks but they did more than edit the book, Moxxy, they got close, very close. I know, I was there."

Moxxanne scoffed. "So what?"

Orson leaned back into the light again and pursed his lips, a kind of satisfaction.

"Like you said about Harry's Mexican girlfriend, maybe it was just rough trade, right?"

"Likely was."

"Yeah, Harry was a pretty determined guy back then. Definitely had communication problems with women. So maybe he had a round of rough trade stuff with your mother or maybe it was even more than that."

"Like what?"

"Maybe like rape."

Chapter 29

It was late, maybe two o'clock in the morning, and she was laden down with the effects of half a dozen beers at Orson's double wide. Together they had killed a twelve pack. Now she was back at her own motel room and staring in the bathroom mirror. Slowly she pulled off the silver blonde wig with all its wavelets and dropped it on the floor. Right away she saw that she was crying, the beginning rivulets of mascara on her cheeks. Plainly she could see her own sadness, the blue green eyes all watery, the downturned lips with the lipstick almost gone. A shudder went through her – the last time she could remember crying was when she was eleven years old.

Her mother, Della Lolly, had just told her the story about the donated sperm, which meant that she was an artificial insemination baby, a donated sperm baby. She'd always been precocious, older than her years. At first this startling news didn't get through, it was just another fabulous yarn that her mother was given to telling her. It was only later, in her own room and hugging her teddy bear that a shudder went through her and she began to weep. That was the exact time that her childhood ended. She knew it – and it was that loss that had brought the tears.

And now she was crying again, in this far from home Gaylord Motel. Her tears were flowing now, and all because this man Orson had told her something completely unsuspecting and strange: that the man she'd always thought of as her Uncle Harry had done a bad thing – he'd raped her mother.

This woeful image in the mirror could not be herself – no – never, never. She raised her clenched fists like hammers and slammed at the mirror again and again – but it refused to break – her image still there, defying her.

She threw herself face down on the bed and after a while the shuddering stopped. It was dark but there was enough window light for her to see the cognac on the dresser. She swung her feet to the floor and grabbed the bottle. No need of a glass, she took a slug and wiped her mouth with the back of her hand.

So what did Orson actually say? She went over it in her head. It was the time of the second Zenith and Orson and Harry were both in Collingwood. Orson was there because he was Harry's friend and general advisor. Harry was there because he had written Zenith, and now it had to be professionally edited – a job that her mother Della Lolly was given to do. Still, the whole thing was a rush job – only two weeks, and Orson said that during that time Harry and her mother were inseparable, and that they did more than edit the book. Orson said that he'd had his suspicions and more or less confirmed little by little when Harry was in his drinks. Truth in booze. Orson had no proof but probably that's what happened. Harry had raped her mother. Orson thought she should know.

So now Moxxanne was left wondering – was she better off being an insemination baby or the result of Harry raping her mother?

Chapter 30

It was ten o'clock in the morning at Harry's not-quite-big-enough-to-be-a-mansion home. The outside temperature was –20°C but inside in Harry's upstairs den it was quite comfortable even though the fireplace was unlit. Harry was behind his big oak writing desk and everything about him said he was a sick old man. He had three or four days of bristly white beard and was weeks past a regular haircut so that lank mostly silver hair hung down his forehead almost covering his eyes. The face itself was sallow and gaunt as well as being creased what with age and his recent hard days. His dark eyes were set in their sockets but this morning they were a little brighter and aware. His terry cloth dressing gown seemed to swallow up Harry's shrunken torso. He'd been letting his cup of coffee cool off just before Moxxanne had arrived.

So there she sat in the comfy chair in front of Harry's desk. Her biker jacket cast to the floor beside the chair. She too was not on her best day, the usually attractive red hair appeared to have barely seen a comb this morning, the green eyes tired like she'd hadn't slept, and no glad smile, the turned down lips almost dour. She was wearing a dark mock turtle that run up her neck and covered down to the wrists. She wore beat up blue jeans and was barefoot, snow boots down by the front door.

"I'm done with all this now," Moxxanne said. "Just give me the third Zenith manuscript and I'll be on my way."

Harry nodded and then pointed to the coffee thermos.

"Kinda sudden, eh? Maybe you'll have a coffee first and tell me what's the hurry."

Moxxanne clasped her hands and slumped in the leather chair. "I'm so goddamned disappointed in you. According to Orson you're just a shit." She shook her head, there may have been tears.

Harry watched her carefully and then picked up his coffee mug with both hands so as not to spill. After, he took a napkin and dubbed at his pale lips. "Orson, eh? Careful now, he's my best friend you know."

Moxxanne sat up. There were no tears and her strong look was back. "He told me stories, Harry, about you and the Mexican girl in Hollywood."

Harry leaned back and pulled his robe around him. He brushed back the flap of dangling hair and rubbed his forehead. It was ten o'clock in the morning and he was already weary.

"The reason Orson is my friend is that I liked him right away. I could see that he's a bit of a wizard – and a mischievous one at that. Maybe the boxing had something to do with it because he's a fabulist who likes to tell enchanting stories. Hell, he shoulda been the writer, not me."

Moxxanne was unimpressed. "Orson said you tried to strangle this Mexican girl and the cops got you."

Harry smiled, the coffee cup warming his hands. "I told you, Orson is mischievous. I wouldn't doubt that he's got some reasons behind this. You see, he did have an involvement with a young actress that was on the Zenith set, and yeah, there was some kind of altercation and the cops got involved but then the whole thing melted away and nothing more came of it. True story."

Moxxanne smiled but it was the smile of disbelief. "Orson said you had trouble with Alva and gave her black eyes."

"Did he now. Well, he's a charming guy and that's why he's my best friend. He's mischievous and he turned that story too. Alva and Orson are practically husband and wife. They've cooled off these days but they used to go toe to toe regularly. Sometimes Orson got the black eye."

Moxxanne thought back to what she knew about Alva – no doubt about it – she could be a tough cookie. But these incidents were trifling compared to what was really on her mind. "Orson told me about how you and he were in Collingwood for the editing of the second Zenith. Seems like he tags along wherever you go."

Harry shrugged. "Orson missed the limelight after he quit boxing and had to go back to the steel mill. I was a steel mill guy too. Then I got lucky with this writing thing and Orson sort of included himself in some of the success I was having. I let him because he was my friend."

Moxxanne eyes didn't soften as she waggled an accusatory finger. "Orson said that you had an affair with my mother."

Harry opened his hands wide. "We did, if you could call it that. I spent a lot of time with her over the editing of Zenith and she was the one who made the story work. Everything I ever got out of Zenith I owe to your mother."

Moxxanne put her elbows on the desk. "It's time for the truth, Harry. Orson says that you're a fuck-up with women. You beat them up. Orson say it was that way with my mother too. Orson says there's a possibility that you might have even raped her."

Harry laced his liver spotted hands together. "I told you, he's a fabulist. Okay, these kind of stories aren't new to me. Don't end up hating the guy. Look, he must have some kind of reason for turning everything around, like he's leading you somewhere. I never had a date with your mother, not outside of the publishing house. But Orson did. You have no idea how charming he could be back then. He was the handsome extrovert, not me."

Moxxanne squinted, her look uncertain. "Wait a goddamned minute. So you're saying Orson was dating my mother?"

Harry shrugged. "Of course he was."

Moxxanne nodded her head slowly. "I'm going to have to kill one of you sonsabitches. I just don't know which one." Moxxanne bit her lip. "Come on, Harry – the truth now – I'm trying to find out about my mother."

Harry's coffee was getting cold and he was feeling tired. He slowly shook his head. "Seems like you've got two different versions of things, Moxxanne. Good, so now you get to choose which story you want."

Moxxanne rose in fury and with the back of her hand swept Harry's coffee mug against the side of the fireplace where it shattered and spattered to the carpet floor. Just as quickly she sat down, sullen, her face nasty.

If Harry was shocked he didn't show it, just nodded wearily and managed a smile. Finally he spoke. "I told you Orson was a very good looking guy back then. He's bald now but back then he had a full head of hair. It was the first thing you noticed about him."

Anger was on Moxxanne's face and she spoke harshly. "Why would that be?"

"You can't tell now but back then it was like yours, a true redhead."

Moxxanne eyes went all wide and her jaw slackened. "You're shittin' me."

"Nope. Funny, isn't it? You've both got the same green eyes too. Didn't you notice that?"

Chapter 31

Moxxanne was wearing her blonde silver wig and her face looked fresh and rested; everything her about said that her old self-confidence was back, smile, the revealing white top, the perfectly fitting jeans with ripped knees and the bare feet with purple painted toenails. She sat on Harry's soft chair that was in front of his oaken desk, Harry in place on his elaborate chair. He was the first to speak.

"Nice surprise. You said you were leaving town, never to see me again. And you're early – it's only 10:00 a.m."

Moxxanne face was enigmatic, the lips a smile and sneer at the same time. She shook her head. "You should know better, Uncle. I'm not leaving until I get the third Zenith so you might as well get it out of your safe and hand it over."

Harry rocked back, he looked a little better this morning but not by much. "So, what did you do with my friend Orson? You confronted him already?"

Now Moxxanne did smirk. "Don't you worry about Orson. I could handle him from day one. You called him a fabulist but so are you – you don't fool me either."

Moxxanne leaned forward and pointed to an unopened letter on Harry's desk.

"My granny's letter. I delivered that the first time I saw you and it's not even opened."

Harry put a shaky hand on the envelope. "I did thank you for bringing it and there's a reason I didn't open it."

"Yeah, like what?"

"Something I'm sure you couldn't know and don't blame Gertrude Bachalder because she probably didn't know either. Just before you arrived I got a call from Roger, my lawyer, telling me that a settlement from Advent Studios was in the offing. He had some ballpark numbers so I made a counter offer. I haven't heard back yet. That's why I didn't open the letter."

Moxxanne shook her head, disbelieving.

"The head guy from Yakushita was right there in Granny's office. That was right before I left. That's when they settled it – except for you. I think it's time you read that letter, Harry. And besides, what were you doing talking to Advent? Did you forget that you're contracted to Patterson Publishing?"

Harry nodded wearily.

"Yakushita runs Advent Studios. You guys know that." He lifted a shaky hand and shook his head. "Roger was talking to Patterson's lawyers, not Advent's. Therefore I had to figure that Patterson Publishing was making me a settlement offer." He opened hands palms outward. "And then you come along with your letter. What's going on, Moxxanne?"

Moxxanne stared, stiffening. "I'm not a lawyer yet but I'm getting there. I smell a legal mix-up and no doubt it's because of Yakushita. They're not even waiting for the ink to dry before they move ahead. Granny's going to be furious."

Harry creaked back in his chair. "Supposing you were my lawyer. What would you advise me to do?"

Moxxanne smiled, a nice bright one. "Easy. Roger knows the settlement numbers by now. Talk to him, then open the letter. If Granny's numbers are lower, then talk to me. I'll make sure you end up with the best numbers. After that, you give me the third Zenith."

Harry nodded and smiled wanly.

"Agreed. Let's call Roger right now."

Chapter 32

Harry's wheelchair creaked, it needed oil, and Harry seemed even more decrepit since their last visit only a few days ago.

"Oh, I think you'll agree," Harry said, voice friendly but weary.

"Agree to what?" Moxxanne said, long fingered hands on the desk top. "There's an alternative here?"

They were sharing a bottle of Gentleman Jack again and Harry's hand shook noticeably as he sipped.

"I'm going to make you an offer that you won't be able to refuse."

This brought a pretty smirk. "Godfather crap."

"I'm going to give you the Zenith manuscript – that's what you want, isn't it?"

"Damned right I do. You said you'd get it out of your safe and have it for me today. Okay, here I am. Let's have it, Uncle Harry."

Harry craggy face was foxy. "There's a catch, nothing you can't handle."

"Strings, eh. Like what?"

Harry creaked back, hand against his lined face. "I've decided to buck the odds and not go gently into that good night after all."

Moxxanne put fingers into her red hair, fluffing it, an aura around her face. "Good for you, Uncle Harry. Hang on as long as you can. These townies have already got you dead and buried."

"With your help I might just do that – put them off for a while. They tell me I've got a fifty-fifty chance."

"Oh? How so?"

"Heart operation but I'd have to go to Vancouver and soon. That's where you come in."

Moxxanne was wearing a mauve cable knit displaying, naturally, cleavage. She tugged the sleeves up to her elbows and clenched her jaw. "Open heart. At this late date?"

"Didn't know 'til recently. Apparently there's a place in the back of my heart that's gone stiff, and it's been draining the life out of me. There's this heart surgeon in Vancouver who learned a new procedure in Rochester and now he needs candidates – to practice on. I volunteered. That is, if you'll come with me."

Moxxanne rocked back, hands on her chest. "Whoa. I'm not up for that. Get yourself a nurse. Take Orson."

"Orson will go, sure, but I need you."

"Oh God. Why me?"

"I told you, I've been waiting two years, ever since my luck went rotten. I knew something would come along and it turned out to be you: my avatar."

"Oh for God's sake, I'm no avatar. What good could I possibly do?"

Tired now and sinking into himself but still smiling grimly.

"Maybe I'm receptive in ways you might not think. For instance, I can feel your energy. Your presence is a power I can draw on. But I'm not asking you to understand it or do anything. Just be there close by. With your strength, I think I can pull the odds around in my favour."

Moxxanne pushed back from the desk.

"Wait a minute," she protested, hands out. "That kind of responsibility I do not need."

Harry shook his head, near the end of his energy. "I told you, you won't have responsibility, none at all. This is not about the operation. It's about my making the decision, making the commitment to go to Vancouver and buck the odds. I want to use you as my talisman, my good luck charm."

His eyelids drooped and then fluttered and there was a plea in his face.

"I need you around so I can get up the guts to get on that airplane and go to Vancouver and face the gamble. The stakes are going to be high. Everything I have on the line."

Moxxanne leaned forward elbows on the desk and they sat a few feet apart.

Harry spoke softly. "I'm telling you up front that you have no responsibility if it goes bad. Your job ends when they roll me into the OR."

Moxxanne reached out and covered the old man's hands.

She too spoke softly. "Maybe it's up to me to decide where my job ends."

Chapter 33

Moxxanne wasn't wearing her fabulous blonde wig. No, she was back to her own more modest red hair which wasn't as long or luxurious but still reached down the nape of her neck and of a shade more orange than auburn. This naturally showed off her best facial feature: her prominent and intelligent light eyes. With her fake hair Moxxanne had a different persona. Along with her height and full figure she became a man stopper while her own natural hair look was that of the more proper ego, the more serious third year law student but the tamer look was still that of an alluring young woman.

She was wearing her sunglasses in their on top-of-the-head position while she stared intently down at the old man in the Vancouver General Hospital bed. She'd been thus for the better part of an hour, this clasping the old man's hand and staring watchfully at his pinched face. The hospital room was private and the door closed so only muted ward sound could be heard. The old man had a tube in his nose as well as a clipped oxygen feed and the requisite IV drip. His eyes were closed and a forelock of grey hair dangled.

Moxxanne gently clenched the old man's hand in both of hers, like she was sending a silent message – wake up, Harry, wake up.

And then there was the other sound, the one she made as she rhythmically chewed her favourite Double Bubble gum, and now she let the pink texture grow beyond her lips, letting it swell and swell into an egg-sized bubble then popped it, an unmistakable smack, and it collapsed across her lower face but did not stick because she was able to wind it back with her tongue. But, the popping noise had done something because Harry's eyes opened.

Moxxanne stopped chewing. Harry's eye flickered, like he was going back under but she gave his hand a hard squeeze. Harry's eyes stared straight up, then began to swing around.

"Harry? It's me, Moxxanne." She bent close so that her red hair touched his face.

Harry licked at his parched lips while his dark eyes sought her, he managed a cough but no words came out, then a faint smile, and at last, "I, I … can smell you … nice."

Moxxanne locked her hands on the old man's "Uncle Harry … you made it. You fooled them all. You did open heart and you're still here."

She put her warm palm on the old man's brow. Then she clasped his hand again.

Harry squeezed back with surprising strength, "Stay close. How long … I'm here?"

"You had surgery all yesterday morning. It's Tuesday afternoon. Dr. Bronson says he fixed you up, Uncle Harry."

"Fixed me?"

"That's what he said."

Harry spoke barely above a whisper. "Maybe … I fly … again."

Then he went back under.

CPSIA information can be obtained
at www.ICGtesting.com
Printed in the USA
LVOW11*1729131117
556109LV00007B/42/P

9 781525 510847